Rustler Roundup

Cord Wheeler, the El Paso detective, finds his services hired by rich cattle dealer Jase Elford for a journey down to Santiago. And all he has to do is act as Elford's bodyguard for the duration of the trip.

But, soon after their arrival in town Elford is murdered and Wheeler finds himself at the centre of a rustling scam. Amidst the killing and corruption, an innocent boy is blamed for Elford's murder and is due to be hanged. Wheeler takes on the deadly task of stopping the rustling gang and exposing their leader, but he'll have to find their secret hideout first.

Locked in a running fight across the badlands, Wheeler must take on the whole gang and win if justice is to be served.

Rustler Roundup

GEORGE J. PRESCOTT

A Black Horse Western

ROBERT HALE · LONDON

© George J. Prescott 2005
First published in Great Britain 2005

ISBN 0 7090 7765 3

Robert Hale Limited
Clerkenwell House
Clerkenwell Green
London EC1R 0HT

Typeset by
Derek Doyle & Associates, Shaw Heath.
Printed and bound in Great Britain by
Antony Rowe Limited, Wiltshire

CHAPTER ONE

Midnight's chill was settling over the dirty streets and alleyways of El Paso's red-light quarter, but the crowd in Boss Kirby's 'High Roller' saloon showed no signs of flagging.

Noise and laughter and the clink of glasses, seasoned by the occasional curse, filled every corner of the bright, ornately decorated room. Well, nearly every corner.

In a large, well-lit alcove, separated from the main room by a flimsy beaded curtain, the silence was almost church-like. Seated facing the entrance so that his eye could reach every corner of the barroom, Boss Kirby looked every inch the rich saloon owner, from his carefully manicured hands to the expensive broadcloth suit that encased his tall, stick-thin frame. He was glaring at the slim man in smoked green glasses and old black suit seated opposite him, his back to the barroom.

'Well, mister?' Kirby snapped abruptly.

For a moment the other appeared not to notice, then he said mildly, 'Raise. Two fifty.'

With a curse, Kirby slammed his bony fists on to the table in front of him and half lurched to his feet. Luck hadn't gone the thin man's way, despite the able administrations of Otis Myers, the house's best mechanic and there was an edge of temper on his words as he said, 'You know I ain't got enough to cover that!' His opponent shrugged slightly.

'Y – Y – You set the rules,' he stammered, his voice a nervous Yankee burr. 'Table stakes. That means, where I come from, what you've got in your pockets. If you can't pay, you can't play.'

In control of himself once more, Kirby settled back into his chair.

'There's a simple solution to this. I'll give you my marker.'

'No.' The voice was flat and somehow the Yankee burr was gone. 'Put up or I take the pot. And I ain't interested in no gold watches, neither.'

Face suffused with temper, Kirby glared down at the cards spread on the green baize surface. The game was five-card stud, with the hole card and two cards dealt. Kirby's hand showed a queen and a ten, both diamonds, with a second queen face down in the hole. His opponent showed a five of clubs and the ace of diamonds. Everything depended on the stranger's hole card.

Indolently, Kirby rubbed his finger gently across the green baize surface in front of him and obedient to the signal, Myers flipped his watch face down, leaving the highly polished back facing upwards. Apparently unnoticed by the other players, Myers lifted the deck and carefully placed it in front of the Easterner, momentarily passing it slowly over the watch so that the bottom card was reflected in the time piece's gleaming surface. Kirby grimaced, fighting to keep the elation from his face. An ace! So the best Mr Fancy Pants Easterner could do was three of a kind.

With renewed confidence, the saloon keeper said, 'I don't much appreciate a man who refuses my marker, but since you insist, here's what I'll do.' He drew a piece of flimsy paper from his pocket and went on, 'I just happen to have this deed in my pocket which I'll sell to you for five thousand dollars.' He tendered the paper and sat back, adding expansively, 'You'll find it's easy worth that.'

Briefly, his opponent studied the document, before throwing it back across the table.

'A thousand,' he said shortly.

'A thousand bucks!' Kirby roared, startled out of his customary equanimity. 'Christ, the house is worth more'n that!'

The Easterner nodded. 'Mebbe,' he said mildly, 'but it ain't worth that here and now. Perhaps one of these gentlemen will accommodate you, since you don't like my offer,' he added, indicating the other players with a sweep of a lean brown hand. There was no reply and the Easterner went on, 'But since it's plain, Mr Kirby, that you ain't used to playing with the big boys, ah'm gonna take it easy on you.' For an instant, the Yankee burr was gone, and the voice had slipped into the slow courtliness of New Orleans. In that instant, memory stirred in Kirby's mind, only to be swept away by blind red rage as his opponent said, 'You accept my offer, I'll deal the rest and let you call me for what's in front of you. And you'll understand them's my children's rates.'

For a moment, skinny hands flexing, Kirby fumed, mastering his temper. But there was still that ace. Finally, he nodded,

'Deal the cards!' Clumsily, the slim man picked up the deck and pausing only to push his glasses further on to his nose, he dealt Kirby a card face up. It was the queen of clubs. Eagerly, the saloon-keeper watched as his opponent flipped his own card. An ace. The slim man paused,

'Well?' he asked, clearly implying that Kirby might have lost his nerve.

'Deal 'em,' Kirby snarled and all but yipped in triumph as the last queen dropped on to his pile. Now the stranger couldn't win, despite the last ace that joined the other two on the hand across the table.

Kirby leaned back, a satisfied smirk disfiguring his yellow, cadaverous face.

'You said something about children's rates before, mister.' He sneered, 'How about we make it a real game?'

The other shrugged. 'What did you have in mind?' he asked mildly. Kirby leaned forward, his face feral in the bright lamp light. 'That ranch you just bought against . . . this,' he snapped, indicating the barroom.

'Boss, you can't . . .' Myers began, but a soft voice was interrupting.

'Done,' the slim man said. 'Make out a paper,' he ordered as he tossed the ranch deed on to the pile.

Kirby scribbled a few brief words and after a quick glance, his opponent dropped the paper on to the heap in the centre of the table and said, 'Turn your card, you ugly bastard.'

The voice was pure New Orleans now and memory was screaming at Kirby as he flipped his hole card face up and sneered, 'Four little ladies, tinhorn.'

'Good,' the other admitted, 'but not good enough. Four l'il bullets sure kills them females.' And the room seemed to reel around Kirby, as the stranger turned his hole card to reveal the fourth ace.

Carefully, the slim man removed his glasses and Kirby found himself looking into a pair of glacial green eyes, while a well-remembered and hated voice was saying softly, 'And just make the ranch over to Mr J Vance, you cheatin' bastard. You remember him? He's the fella you stole it from.'

For an instant, Boss Kirby seemed frozen, rooted to his chair, face working apoplectically. Then he screamed. The scream was a single word and the word was a name,

'Wheeler!' And even as the scream left his lips, Kirby was moving. His left hand flipped the table away from him while his right was driving for the little derringer in its waistband holster. He jerked the little weapon free, hesitating slightly as he tried to line the pistol on his intended target. But he waited too long. Cord Wheeler hadn't risen from his chair but the big bore Smith & Wesson was in his hand and roaring an instant before Kirby could make up his mind to fire.

Wheeler's first shot sliced into the thin man's chest, killing him instantly and even as he fought the heavy weapon's recoil, Wheeler jerked forward, dodging the razor in Otis Myers' hand and triggering his second shot into the card-sharp's exposed knee cap.

Myers collapsed, screaming and clutching his ruined knee, while Wheeler snapped erect, turning smoothly to face the barroom.

And that was how Birdy Johnstone, arriving seconds later clutching a sawn-off that he hoped desperately he wouldn't have to use, found himself looking down the barrel of Wheeler's Smith & Wesson, as a cold Louisiana voice said mildly, 'Now just put that gun down, Mr Johnstone, afore you hurt yourself. Besides,' the soft, icy voice went on, 'you're gonna be busy . . . now you've got your place back.'

And out in the barroom, a tanned, well-built rancher, dressed in a good broadcloth suit and hand-made Texas boots, paused in his questioning of the bartender to listen. Someone, somewhere was whistling 'Shenendoah'.

This same individual was shown, the following morning, into Cord Wheeler's office by an impressed Mollie Simpson. While the man was seating himself, she whispered, 'Cord, try not to upset this one. He looks like he might have money.'

Smilingly, Wheeler ushered out the unwilling Mollie and, upon returning, found his visitor already seated and puffing on an expensive Havana.

Without preamble the other began, 'Name's Elford, Mr Wheeler, Jase Elford. I'm a cattle buyer, work mostly out of San Antonio.'

'You don't sound like a Texan,' Wheeler offered mildly. Elford laughed, although his eyes narrowed nervously.

'You're right,' he chuckled, 'but you gotta be where

the cows are. Anyhow, what I'm here for is 'cause I got a deal that's soured up on me.' Wheeler made no reply and Elford went on, 'A while ago, I sold some cows to a rancher, name o' Cal Underwood. Lives near a place on the border called Santiago. He was short o' coin, so I took his six month note fer the critturs. Six months is up, so I aim to collect.'

'Cow buyers usually deal strictly for cash,' Wheeler said.

Elfords' eyes flickered nervously but he raised a strained laugh as he admitted, 'Yeah, I know, but I done business with Underwood for years an' I figgered he was good for it.' Wheeler simply nodded and with this minimal encouragement, Elwood continued, 'Now I figger to go down to this one horse piss hole that he calls a ranch and get my money ... some way. But Underwood might turn mean, him or his boys, so I figger to take some high quality help and Mr Wheeler, you were recommended to me as the best there is, with a gun or knife. And after what I seen in the High Roller last night, I can believe it!'

'It ain't called the High Roller any more,' Wheeler said. 'Mr Johnstone is going rename it the Busted Four Flusher in memory of the late and unlamented Mr Kirby.'

'What exactly come off there last night?' Elford asked.

'About six months ago, Kirby comes to town with a gamblin' outfit,' Wheeler began. 'He sets up business on Main Street and the other places in town start havin' bad luck. Couldn't get liquor, mysterious fires, that kind o' thing. One by one they sell out to Kirby or

11

go bust. Last of all he gets Johnstone's place for a song after the bank closes on Birdy's mortgage.' Wheeler shifted slightly. 'Then he starts collectin' ranches. He cheated a young fella Mollie and Ira are fond of, night before last, and Mollie told me to get his ranch back. Simple.' Wheeler shrugged in conclusion.

'And how was he so sure he had you beat, that you never had that last ace?'Elford demanded.

'He was a good poker player,' Wheeler admitted, 'but he tried to be too clever. It don't never pay to be too clever, Mr Elford,' Wheeler finished.

Elford had been gone some hours, having departed with an assurance that Wheeler would accept his proposition, when, with evening falling, the detective eased himself into his customary place at Mollie Simpson's spotless kitchen table. Her husband Ira was already there.

Wheeler began without preamble. 'You ever heard of a cattle buyer workin' in Texas, who'd take a six month note for a lot of cows?'

'Them Texicans won't even take Federal green backs!' Ira laughed explosively. 'And, as you well know, no cow dealer gives credit on account of, if he ain't got money, he can't do business. No,' Ira finished soberly, 'man wants to buy cows, he takes out a mortgage for the cash. No cow dealer'll take a rancher's note. Why'd you ask?'

'Fella come to see me today about a job,' Wheeler began and when he'd finished his account of Elford's visit, Ira Simpson leaned back in the plain wooden chair.

12

'It stinks,' he said simply.

'It sure does,' Mollie agreed, having come in halfway through the story.

'You ain't goin', are you, Cord?' she demanded as she watched Wheeler counting a pile of bills he had taken from his pocket.

'Now, Mollie honey, I can't take the nice man's money and not turn up. Especially on account of him offerin' me a thousand bucks for ten days' work,' Wheeler said teasingly.

'If you weren't sure before,' Simpson put in, 'that thousand would tell you this job ain't what he says. That's five times the rate for the job.'

'Mebbe he thinks I'm worth it.' Wheeler shrugged. ' 'Sides I need the money to keep Mollie in fancy doodads,' he finished, passing most of the notes across the table to his friend's wife.

'Pay off some of Ira's gamblin' buddies,' he whispered to her behind his hand.

For a moment Mollie glared at him, before snapping, 'I'll put it in the bank under your name, along with the rest, so you might just get something back for all the risks you take! God knows you ought to get something!' she finished waspishly, even though Wheeler could see that she was plainly close to tears.

'I've got somethin', Mollie darlin',' Wheeler said slowly, although the green eyes watching her were very gentle as he stood and flexed his long, steely fingers.

'What?' she snapped abruptly, glaring up at him.

'What have I got?' he repeated softly, almost to himself. 'Why, I've got the next job.'

CHAPTER TWO

'Sure glad the stage company don't charge for the dust,' the old man sitting next to Wheeler offered whimsically, 'I musta ate near on a pound.' Wheeler nodded in sympathy as the coach pulled to the top of the last rise and the driver leaned on his reins, pausing to let his team breathe and gather them for the final long descent.

'Santiago down yonder, folks,' the driver offered but Wheeler made no move to follow as the old man and the plain middle-aged woman who was the vehicle's only other passenger craned their necks to look. He'd been in enough of these hole-in-the-wall border towns to know exactly what he'd see. The single street with its mixture of clapboard and adobe buildings, the flies and the stink. It'd all be there soon enough.

And Santiago did its best not to disappoint him as Wheeler stepped down from the stage. The smell, if anything was worse than any place he remembered being, composed of a mixture of horse and rank human with something that might have been goat. Greaser cooking added its own individual harmony to the stink.

Wheeler's nose wrinkled involuntarily as he brushed fastidiously at the front of the old duster coat he was wearing. Leaning heavily on his brass-handled stick, he reached up for his battered carpet-bag and, as the guard tendered it, the man said kindly, 'It ain't none o' my never mind, mister, but if I was you, I'd get my business done and get out o' here.'

Wheeler looked his question and after glancing round nervously, the other went on, 'There's some rough *hombres* around here, so just watch yourself, is all.'

'Thanks for the advice,' Wheeler said smilingly. 'I'll sure bear it in mind.' Turning awkwardly, the man from El Paso began to limp heavily in the direction of the town's only hotel. Following his route, the guard's gaze swept on to take in the group leaning on the hitch rail at the front of that building and what he saw there caused him to draw in his breath sharply, with an abrupt head shake.

Wheeler had apparently not noticed the little group by the rail, but as he put his foot on the first step leading up to the well-swept porch, a cocky voice said, 'Hey, mister, you better git someone to tote that heavy bag fer you.' Wheeler stepped away from the porch and turned slowly to find himself looking at a tall, thickset youngster, dressed in range clothes, with a pair of pearl-handled Colts holstered at his side. As Wheeler's amused gaze swept the little group, one of the others grabbed the big youngster's arm.

'C'mon Billy, let's get us a drink. No cause to beat up on no cripple.' Without deigning to look at his friend, Billy shoved the other away from him, sending the boy sprawling in the dust.

'Now see, mister, bag totin' comes expensive around here. Cost you five dollars to get that bag delivered into that there hotel,' Billy explained, jerking his head towards the doorway.

Idly, Wheeler shifted the cane under his right hand, bringing his left up to grasp the stick at its point of balance.

'Now, this's been fun and I sure appreciate the reception committee,' he began mildly, 'but looks to me like time for you boys to run along home and get Ma to change your diapers.' Idly, he glanced up at the sun, 'Must be about time for your nap, too.'

With a nasty grin, Billy turned slowly towards his friends, expressively spreading his hands, before jerking back towards Wheeler abruptly, swinging up a meaty fist.

In one deceptively smooth movement, Wheeler ducked under the clumsy punch and, as Billy overbalanced and made to stumble past him, the detective smashed the lead-weighted brass handle of his stick into the big cowboy's temple. Limp as a pole-axed steer, Billy collapsed on to hands and knees, shaking his head to clear it. He needn't have bothered because in a lightning quick continuation of his first move, Wheeler's neatly shod left foot lashed out, catching his opponent under the chin and depositing the half-conscious cowboy into the dusty street.

Dribbling blood and curses in about equal measure, Billy pushed himself up as he desperately clawed for one of the fancy Colts. Wheeler's pistol

16

was already in his left hand and he was debating cynically how many of these stupid kids he'd end up having to shoot before they realized he was serious, when there was the blast of a shotgun. Dust erupted a bare six inches from Billy's leg and a pleasant feminine voice was saying, 'That'll be enough, boys. You've had your fun. Now git before Mr Wheeler here has to shoot someone.'

A single snatched glance showed Wheeler a statuesque, middle-aged woman who handled the sawn-off she held as though it wasn't the first time she'd done something like this. Impatient at the lack of response from Wheeler's victim, she lifted the weapon and said clearly, 'You know what I got this loaded with, don't you, Billy? Rock salt and bird shot,' she continued, without waiting for a response. 'And you know where I'm gonna be aimin', don't you? Oh, it won't kill you but you sure won't feel like sampling none of Uncle John's merchandise fer a while.'

There was a moment's pause then a rat-faced cowboy at the back of the group sneered, 'What d'you say, Billy? Mebbe the dude can't shoot.'

Without any appearance of being aimed, the Smith & Wesson in Wheeler's hand cracked once and the rat-faced one's sombrero leapt from his head and skittered down the street.

'That's the only one I'm wasting, boys,' Wheeler stated icily. 'Now you go play somewhere else.'

'They didn't mean no harm, Mr Wheeler,' the woman assured him, as she proffered the register for

17

his signature. Billy had been half carried, half dragged away by his friends, leaving Wheeler to continue his quest for a room.

'El Paso,' she noted, as she examined his entry. 'I hear it's a nice town, although I've never been there myself.'

'Why sure, ma'am,' Wheeler agreed, 'I live on Fargo Street, down near the docks, opposite the old Forty-Niner saloon.'

'The Forty-Niner ain't in . . .' she began, then caught herself. 'I mean,' she went on, with barely a pause, 'ain't that an interesting name, Mr Wheeler? I suppose it has to do with the gold-rush days?'

'Guess so, ma'am,' Wheeler admitted, with a slow nod, having apparently not noticed her slip. 'Guess I'll leave my gear and mebbe take in the town.' The woman nodded. 'Dinner at seven sharp, if you'd like to eat here, Mr Wheeler,' she called to his retreating back.

Safely ensconced in his room, Wheeler locked the door and having propped a chair under the handle, removed his coat. He stretched briefly. Faking the limp was hard work, especially remembering always to favour his right leg.

In the early days, when he first discovered that a limp and a mild manner put people off their guard and meant they would talk to an inoffensive crippled detective, whatever questions he asked, he'd once slipped and begun limping on the left. Cord Wheeler shook his head at the memory. Julio's boy, Enzo Casino, had been quick to notice and even quicker to put two and two together and make five. Fortunately, he had shouted a warning to his boss in the big barroom of that same Forty-Niner saloon instead of simply shooting first, and Wheeler had blown his head off almost before the words were out of his mouth and his pistol had cleared its holster. His lover Julio, died a split second later, but not before he had managed to puncture the fleshy part of Wheeler's forearm, leaving a scar that still ached in cold weather.

Absently, Wheeler rubbed at the corded tissue beneath his worn shirt, before abruptly jerking his mind back to the present.

Without thinking, he broke open the Smith & Wesson and replaced the spent cartridge, his hands doing the work automatically, while his mind pondered the paradox of Mariah Keely.

That she had been in El Paso was plain, as was the fact that, whatever she'd been doing, the ladies of the Moral Guardians' League probably wouldn't have approved. Of course, Wheeler reminded himself acidly, it wasn't a crime to have secrets in your past that you weren't proud of, but just the same. . . .

Abruptly, he gave the cylinder of his revolver a final twirl, before slipping it into the stiff, greasy holster and picking up his stick.

Stepping softly, he slipped through the door, wedging a tiny shard of cigarette paper between the door and its frame as he eased the door shut. Reaching down, his sensitive fingers found the marker but when he stepped back, the tiny brown slip was invisible. Wheeler grimaced. It wasn't meant to be that sort of job, but a man lived longer if he

19

didn't neglect the precautions.

Santiago's only saloon was a plain single-storey adobe which sprawled untidily back from the main street. Wheeler pushed through the peeling swing doors, into the cool of the barroom, to find its only occupants to be a yawning bartender and an old man energetically pushing a broom across the clean, sanded floor.

Neither man noted the detective's presence and the bartender, broad of stomach, chuckled and said, 'What's your hurry, Sly? Got to see your lady friend agin?'

Pausing to lift his broom the old man said waspishly, 'Willie, if'n your brains was dynamite you wouldn't have enough to blow your hat off. Howdy, mister,' the old man continued, as Wheeler limped away from the door. Wheeler nodded his greeting, propping his stick and hooking a heel on to the brass rail as he did so.

'Tequila,' he said in answer to the bartender's inevitable question, before going on, 'Have one yourself.' And, as the dispenser of drinks poured himself a modest dose, Wheeler raised his voice to the old man's retreating back.

'Excuse me, sir,' he offered politely, 'will you take something with me?' For a moment, the old man paused, then he turned, a look of disbelief etched on his face, as though he and simple courtesy had been strangers too long. A single look at Wheeler's frank smile must have convinced him, however, because he dropped the broom abruptly and strode up to the bar with the swinging bow-legged walk of a long-time horseman.

Pausing before his glass, the old man proffered a hand and said, 'Sylvester Templeton, sir, at your service, and before I drink your liquor, it behoves me to tell you that I am currently without the necessary funds to stand you a return treat. To wit, sir, I'm broke 'til pay day.' The voice was old-time Virginia and Wheeler fought down his smile, understanding and liking a man who wouldn't presume on a stranger's kindness, however near the chuckline he might be.

'Don't give it a thought,' Wheeler assured the old man, giving his own name as he signalled for a refill. 'I guess I'll be here come pay day.'

Wheeler touched lips to his glass, without tasting, and said, 'Good cattle country around here, seems like?'

'Likely enough,' the old man agreed. 'Hereford longhorn crosses do right well hereabouts, long as you can water 'em through the dry spells.' The bartender nodded agreement, as the old man went on darkly, 'Though, o'course, you gotta watch out for vermin.'

Wheeler looked his puzzlement. 'Mite far south for any real wolf trouble, ain't it?' he offered diffidently.

The old man gave a snort of laughter and Willie, the bartender, explained. 'He means two legged vermin. Rustlers.'

Wheeler nodded his understanding as the old man went on, 'Damn skunks. I'd string up every last one. And we would too, if'n we had a marshal who was worth a damn.'

'Ranches losing much?' Wheeler enquired mildly.

'Just enough to make 'em sore,' Templeton answered. 'Jesse Wrawlings, he's manager and part owner of the O Bar O, has got his boys riding their north line with saddle guns across their pommels and he swears he's gonna swing every rustling son of a bitch he catches. He'll do it, too. Jesse's a Texican and about as good a man as you'll find anywhere, but losin' cows is kinda annoyin' to that breed.'

'Enough to annoy anyone,' Wheeler admitted. 'Say, I'm waitin for someone, might be he lives around here, name o' Jase Elford. Would either o' you gents know him?'

'Elford? Cattle dealer, ain't he, does some contract drivin', that the fella?' Templeton demanded, after a moment's thought.

'I didn't know about him driving cows,' Wheeler admitted. 'But fella I'm dealin' with is sure a cow buyer. He live around here?'

'Naw, leastwise not permanent. Got a ranch about forty mile out, down the valley,' came the surprising answer. 'It ain't much, about twenty thousand acres of sand and scrub. Runs a few cows but mostly he uses it for a stop over. You know,' the old man continued, led on by Wheeler's pretended lack of understanding, 'a place to feed and water, fatten the beeves up fer the rest o' the drive. Good place fer it,' the old man acknowledged. 'Near a couple o' the big drive trails fer Fort Worth and the Kansas rail heads, and handy to push beef to the Apache reservation down south,' the old man finished.

'And the Army don't look close at the cows they buy, long as they get 'em fer the right price,' Wheeler mused softly, half to himself.

CHAPTER THREE

Despite spending the entire evening in the saloon, Wheeler saw nothing of his employer, although he did learn a good deal about Elford in his absence. Most of his business seemed to be done down south and previously, Santiago had held no attraction for him, not even as a place to replenish his supplies. Nor did his drive crews drink there, and the only inhabitants of the town who seemed to have any contact with them were range riders like Sly Templeton and the middle-aged cow hand who told Wheeler bluntly, when the detective asked about Elford's men, 'Town ain't missin' nothin'. I seen a few salty crews in my time and Elford's boys look as bad as any of 'em. 'Specially that trail boss o' hisn!'

All in all, Wheeler had a lot to think about as he made his way back to Mariah Keely's boarding-house later that night.

He'd avoided the tequila bottle after treating Templeton, but somehow the streets of the little Mexican town got him mixed and it was late when he found himself trudging up the narrow side alley that faced the back of the boarding-house.

Suddenly, Wheeler stiffened and slid sideways into an area of darker shadow, ears straining. It came again, louder now, the little warning jingle of rowel against spur as its owner moved cautiously into the lighter frame of the alleyway.

Silhouetted against the moon, Wheeler could just make out the giant bulk and two guns of his opponent of the afternoon. Oblivious of Wheeler's presence, Billy slipped out of the shadows and across to the back door of Mariah Keely's boarding-house. He scratched softly and after a moment, the door opened, revealing the boarding-house owner in a négligé that certainly hadn't come from any Sears and Roebuck dream book. The door slammed shut, leaving Wheeler to his own thoughts and the darkness.

None of the previous night's experiences was sufficient, however, to interfere with Wheeler's appetite nor remove the bland expression from his face as he left the tiny dining room after an excellent breakfast, early next day.

Passing the morning greeting to Mariah Keely, busy behind the reception desk, he paused to one side of the doorway as he scanned the street.

Satisfied at last, he stepped out into the shade of the porch.

'Mornin', stranger,' said a hard voice from a chair at the end of the shady veranda and, turning awkwardly, Wheeler saw the substantial figure of Jase Elford.

Nodding his greeting, Wheeler limped along the veranda and all but flopped into the seat next to his client. Awkwardly, he stretched his leg across the boards and began to massage the thigh.

'Trouble?' Elford asked.

'Had a l'il run in with some 'punchers yesterday.' Wheeler shrugged. 'Leg allus acts up if I put any strain on it.'

'Must be hard, being crippled up,' Elford remarked unsympathetically, and the detective didn't miss the malicious gleam in the pale eyes.

'Don't worry about me, Elford,' Wheeler snapped, playing up to his role of resentful cripple, 'I can cut it.'

'Sure, sure you can,' Elford offered, all but patting the detective's shoulder, 'but we gotta be careful. Underwood's got this town sewn up,' he finished and Wheeler hid a grim smile. The role of cripple was a useful one, not least because now Elford, like so many before, had clearly started to underestimate him.

'All right, we better get down to cases,' Elford began, settling comfortably into his chair. 'Better if no one sees us gettin' too friendly, so you walk across to the saloon. Take it nice and easy and I'll meet you there and explain what you gotta do.' Unaccountably, he looked back to the doorway of the boarding house before sneering, 'This place's got too many ears.'

Rising awkwardly, Wheeler stumped down the veranda steps, but the man from El Paso had barely reached the centre of the dusty street, when the slim figure of a girl emerged from the doorway of the store which stood next to the cantina. She was young, barely out of her teens with short blonde hair that all but sparkled with health, unhindered by the battered Stetson that hung by its storm strap, cowboy fashion, down the back of her faded shirt.

Careless of the picture she made, she laughed and called something through the doorway of the store as she ducked under the hitch rail, tightened her mount's girth, then swung aboard the stocky Texas pony.

Before she could settle herself or even grab up the reins, the wiry little animal seemed to explode. Jerking back from the rail, he whirled and snapped his teeth a bare inch from the girl's Levi-clad leg.

Mad with rage, he lunged forward, bucking and sunfishing but from the girl there was never a cry. Teeth gritted, she reached down, almost losing her seat but managing to snatch up the trailing rein. Wrapping the rawhide round her fist, she leaned back hard, sawing on the pony's mouth, desperately trying to bring his head up to where she could grab the other rein.

It might have worked too, but her muscular jerk proved too much for the overworked leather and the rein snapped.

Slamming his head forward, the pony prepared to let rip again, only to find his ear and neck clamped in a vice-like grip so that the weight of his attacker kept his feet on the ground, and the girl heard a cold, abrupt voice ordering, 'Get off him, ma'am, and do it right quick!'

Swiftly, she slipped the stirrups and threw herself bodily sideways, rolling into the dust of the street like a horse breaker, and coming to her feet in almost the same movement.

Relieved of the girl's weight, the little mustang jerked savagely upwards as Wheeler let go his hold, smoothly swinging his body away from the maddened pony.

He needn't have bothered because instead of rising to attack, the beast simply stood, shaking from head to foot, whinnying pitifully and swinging his head to jerk at the saddle on his back.

'Be careful, mister,' girl warned, as Wheeler moved forward, apparently oblivious to the tall young man who stood, open-mouthed in the doorway of store and an older, rat-faced cowboy, leaning on the hitch rail of the saloon, convulsed with laughter.

Moving warily and crooning the meaningless sounds that every cowboy uses and every ranch-trained horse knows comes from a friend, Wheeler gently grasped the pony's bridle. For a full minute he talked and rubbed at the little animal's muzzle, gently soothing, before calling the girl to hold her mount's head.

Still moving gently and crooning to the horse, he reached up and with swift, gentle movements removed saddle and blanket.

What he saw there drew a swift intake of breath and flicked a red light into the Arctic green eyes.

Embedded in the skin of the back were half-a-dozen pieces of choya, the vicious, steel-spiked cactus of the South-West. Placed gently on the animal's back, under a loose saddle, the pony would feel nothing. Tighten the girth and climb aboard and the rider's weight would drive the vicious spines deep into flesh, inflicting unspeakable agony and driving the most docile mount into a furious temper.

'Christ,' came a voice from behind Wheeler, as the detective opened his battered Barlow knife and began to gently pry out the deeply embedded choya. 'Who in hell'd do a thing like that?'

'Ssh, gently, Bubbles,' the girl crooned softly, but there was no softness in her voice as she rounded on the tall youngster. 'You know who the hell it was, Luther Underwood,' she raged. 'That rat-faced Ferris, who rides for the O Bar O. I bet Jesse Wrawlings put him up to it!' She paused for breath, as Wheeler snapped his knife closed one-handed, while he juggled the glistening spikes he'd extracted in the other.

'You must think me very rude and ungrateful, Mister . . .' she began.

'Wheeler, ma'am, Cord Wheeler,' the detective acknowledged, 'and you've had a l'il mite of things on your mind, so I guess you can be excused,' he finished whimsically.

'I'm Delia Underwood and this,' she said, indicating the tall, young cowboy who had been in the doorway of the store, her tone a mixture of anger and affection, 'is my brother Luther. We all call him Lou,' she explained, but it was to Wheeler's departing back.

'Wait up, Mr Wheeler,' she panted, hurrying in the wake of the rapidly limping detective. 'Where you goin' in such an all fired hurry?'

Wheeler's smile was wintry as he said over his shoulder, 'I gotta see a man about a horse.'

The barroom was deserted apart from a group of cowboys gathered at the far end, clustered around a group of tables, apparently bracing themselves for the monthly pay day celebration.

Without comment, Wheeler limped up to the group and held out the choya.

'Know what this is?' he asked mildly, of no one in particular.

'Cotton candy,' a voice sneered from the back of the group. The cowboys parted as Wheeler moved through them to find himself facing the cowboy from the street, the same rat-faced individual who had questioned Wheeler's shooting the day before.

'Did you put this on that pony's back?' Wheeler asked softly, dropping the choya to the floor.

Fooled by his questioner's apparent mildness, Ferris shrugged and laughed.

'Sure,' he admitted, 'Miz high and mighty Underwood. She needed takin' down and I'm saying that's just what I done!' He leaned forward, treating Wheeler to the smell of unwashed body and cheap whiskey.

'What do you think of tha—' Whatever else he had to say was lost to posterity, because, without warning Wheeler slammed the knob of his lead weighted cane up and just under the rat-faced one's rib cage.

Caught precisely in the solar plexus, Ferris jerked forward, momentarily unable to breathe, to be caught smoothly under the lapels of his dirty vest, flipped off his run down boots and deposited neatly on to the spikes of the upturned choya.

Watching the man's desperate attempts to free himself from the cactus, Wheeler turned to the watchful group behind him, looking directly at a big, silver-haired cowboy standing at the front of the crowd, large callused hands hooked into a gunbelt, near the worn black butts of his holstered Colts.

'I've had more hosses than a few die under me, working, and I've even had to eat a couple, but no one ill treats or abuses a pony in my sight,' he said flatly. 'And when that sonofabitch gets the spikes outa his arse, tell him from me, he can consider hisself lucky. There's Texas men I've rode with who'd ha' shot him like the coyote he is for a rotten stunt like that.'

'What d'we do, Pa?' snapped a younger, thinner version of the silver-haired cowboy. 'He's one of our boys! You just gonna let this fancy pants put this over?'

Slowly, the big man turned and something in his face made the youngster blanch and lick his lips. But the boy was game and he rallied, shoving his fists on to his hips and snapping, 'If'n you're scared, Pa, I'll take him.'

As if weary, the older man shoved his Stetson to the back of his head and said patiently, 'Son, he'd have you for breakfast and never know he'd eaten.'

Turning back to Wheeler, the old man went on, 'You shouldn't have done that, mister,' Reaching down, he jerked the hapless Ferris effortlessly to his feet.

'You all right, boy?' he enquired gently, still holding the man by his greasy lapel.

'Sure, boss,' the cowboy slurred.

'Good,' the old man murmured, then slammed his fist under the cowboy's short ribs, following up with a crashing blow to the chin that travelled no more than eight inches and deposited the cowboy in an untidy pile, several feet away at the end of the bar. He turned back to Wheeler, who was nodding appreciatively.

'I told you, you shouldn't have done that. Only what I meant was, you shouldn't ha' done that, 'cause you didn't hit the bastard hard enough,' the old man finished bluntly.

'Pay thet off,' he ordered, turning to his grinning offspring. 'Let him have his saddle but he don't even borry no O Bar O pony.' He turned back to Wheeler, thrusting out a hand like a ham.

'Name's Wrawlings, Jesse Wrawlings,' he offered. 'Yonder's my boy, Davy. I'm right obliged to you, mister, and I'm hopin' you'll oblige me further by acceptin' a drink.'

CHAPTER FOUR

As Wheeler slowly climbed the stairs to his room late that night, he found it hard to suppress a smile at the events of the day.

Jesse Wrawlings' idea of a drink didn't stop short of a bottle, although Wheeler's share was now mixed inextricably with the sand covering the saloon's floor. He'd quickly developed a liking for the shrewd old man and his son Davy, just home from three years in a Wyoming agricultural college.

'Awful smart, that boy o' mine,' Wrawlings confided. 'Got a lot o' bang up ideas. Some look like they'll work an' some,' – he tapped the side of his big, beaky nose – 'I ain't so sure about. But the boy's gotta run his string. Only way he'll learn, from his own mistakes.'

'He won't make many,' Wheeler assured the old man, having made his own assessment of the young man's character. 'And them he does make he'll fix hisself, without squawking. He's the sort this country needs,' he finished, with simple truth.

Wrawlings sighed. 'I'm hopin' he's gonna get the chance,' he admitted. Wheeler looked his question, and the old man went on, 'We got some rustlin' trouble hereabouts, Cord, and I can't rightly get my mind around it.'

'Rustlin' ain't usually complicated.' Wheeler shrugged. 'Cows get stole, and the rustlers drive 'em where they can be sold. They usually work careful, take a few at a time but even then, if'n you got a crew that knows their business and is workin' for you, it's risky, 'cause, sooner or later, someone cuts one o' their drive trails, then you and the boys follow it to their hideout and jist naturally clean house, regardless. But I ain't tellin' you anythin' you don't know already, am I?' he finished.

'No, you ain't,' Jesse Wrawlings admitted. 'My boys, apart from that sidewinder Rat, are good and wise to their work.' He stretched widely, before carefully picking up his full whiskey glass and appearing to examine it in the light of a nearby window.

'And come last roundup, figgerin' natural increase and such, me an' my *segundo*, Jed,' Wrawlings went on, indicating a small, bow-legged cowboy at the further end of the bar, without once taking his eyes from the contents of the glass he held, 'figure we're down upwards of a thousand head for the year. And I'll tell you somethin' else,' Wrawlings finished, ignoring Wheeler's incredulous whistle, 'there ain't no sign of a drive trail anywhere.'

The man from El Paso was still turning over the novel problem of a rustling operation without a drive trail as he stepped up on to the landing of the floor on which his room lay, but what he saw there drove

33

all thought of Wrawlings' troubles from his mind. Now ingrained habit took over, the habit of a man who lives all the days of his life with danger a hair's breadth away.

Moving carefully, Wheeler wedged his cane in the rickety banister, in just the place where a man's foot would descend if he was looking to get down the stairs quickly in the dark.

Eyes fixed on the doorway of his room, he slipped quietly across to the oil lamp above the stairway and turned it to a faint glow. Still moving in perfect silence, he eased up to the door of his room and felt cautiously at the jamb. His slip of paper was missing and he stooped silently, feeling across the floor where he thought he had seen his marker from the top of the stairs.

In a moment, his fingers encountered the flimsy shard. Thrusting it away, he noiselessly drew the Smith & Wesson and reached for the door handle.

A sharp twist and careful shove sent the door swinging inwards as Wheeler's voice snapped from the darkness of the passage.

'Whoever you are, come out with your hands up, now!'

His only answer was silence and Wheeler licked nervously at rapidly drying lips. Either the room was empty or someone was lying in the darkness waiting for him to make the first move and the detective was acutely aware that lying flat on his face in the hotel corridor left him at a distinct disadvantage.

Listening hard, Wheeler allowed a full minute to pass, while he strained his ears in to the enveloping darkness of his room. Nothing stirred.

Moving silently, Wheeler drew up his legs, under his body, before abruptly catapulting himself through the opening and into the well of darkness within. No sign or shot came and it was a rueful Cord Wheeler who got stiffly to his feet minutes later, not, however, before he'd checked every inch of the floor to satisfy himself that the room was empty. Feeling slightly foolish, he collected his cane from the stairway and silently closed and secured the door after him, reminding himself sharply in passing that a man had to be alive to feel foolish, which same he wouldn't be if he neglected basic precautions.

Leaving the room in complete darkness, he moved to the window and inched down the dirty linen blind. More than a few men in his line of work had died because they gave themselves away with an abrupt or careless movement, even something as innocuous as drawing a window blind.

Still not satisfied, he lifted the lamp and placed it behind the room's only easy chair, before carefully lighting it.

Now he had enough light to see, but his silhouette would not appear on the room's light-coloured blind, no matter where he stood. Working swiftly, he drew the dusty, moth-eaten curtains, checking carefully to ensure that no chink of light could escape, before finally lifting the lamp and placing it back on its table in front of the window.

He had barely finished his precautions when there was a sharp tap at the door and a muffled voice demanded, 'Wheeler! Cord Wheeler! Open up, it's me.' The muffled voice seemed familiar but Wheeler was in no mood to take chances. Swiftly blowing out the lamp, he dropped silently on to his belly and shuffled across to the door.

Silently, he turned the key, then crouched back against the wall, easing the tiny, razor-sharp stiletto from its wrist sheath as he did so.

The little blade with its filigree carving was older than Wheeler by many years and it had come to him in blood, on a forgotten battlefield more years ago than he cared to remember. He always thought of the deadly little weapon as 'she' and her only purpose was death by stealth and in silence. She had taken many lives in Wheeler's service.

He lifted the six-inch blade carefully, chest high to take a standing man cleanly in the kidney or lung and said softly, slurring his voice like one tired or drunk, 'Come in.'

Noisily, the door swung back to reveal a tall broad figure in the doorway, and Jase Elford's voice snapped abruptly, 'What in hell's comin' off here? Wheeler, where in hell are you?' But by the time the words had left Elford's mouth, Wheeler had sheathed his blade and slid across the room to the bed, drawing the Smith & Wesson as he did so.

Silently, he slipped on to the cover before deliberately tipping the empty whiskey bottle he had left there on to the floor.

'Wassamarrer,' Wheeler demanded, voice slurring.

'Goddammit,' Elford snapped, 'I hate a drunk wuss'n a cripple and now I'm payin' fer both.' A match scratched and light flooded the room only to dim amd broaden as Elford touched the wick of the grubby lamp.

'Who's 'at,' Wheeler demanded, although a rapidly taken glance had assured him that Elford was alone in the room and that the corridor outside was empty.

'It's me,' Elford snapped, 'the guy who's payin' your wages!'

'Sure, sure,' Wheeler mumbled, swinging his legs off the bed and concealing the heavy revolver under a fold of blanket in the same movement. 'I ain't drunk,' the detective went on, 'just a l'il celebration with some friends of mine.'

'You kin drink yourself to death fer all I care,' Elford snapped, 'I ain't gonna need you, anymore.' Misinterpreting Wheeler's quizzical look, Elford said, 'No, it ain't nothin' to do with this! I found out some-thin',' he sneered, relishing the moment, 'somethin' that gives me the winnin' hand.'

'Here's your coin, includin' for tomorrow though I can't see you done much for it,' he stated arro-gantly.

'I'm gonna see Mr Underwood tonight, then I got a little business in town,' he went on, apparently stung by Wheeler's carefully studied yawn. 'I've cabled my boys, so they'll be here in a day or two. Then I'll settle accounts ... with everybody,' he finished. Turning from the door, Elford sneered, 'You might want to be somewhere else by then ... case my boys decide to get my money's worth some other way.'

Habit drove Wheeler to the door, listening to be

sure that Elford was really on his way, before he turned back happily to bed. Once, after prison and the death of his wife had driven him close to losing his mind, Elford's accusation would have been true. Now, it had been many years since Wheeler had touched a drink, rather becoming adept at spilling his portion to the floor or bar unseen.

Wearily, he eased off his boots and began to unbutton the worn cotton shirt that Mollie had despairingly mended, all the while vociferously berating Wheeler because it was more darns than shirt. He grinned at her memory, carefully placed the Smith & Wesson where his hand would naturally fall to it in the darkness and climbed into bed. He lay back, hands comfortably behind his head. Someone had searched his room that night, obviously while he had been in the cantina. But who?

Mentally, Wheeler shrugged. There was one obvious candidate but suspicions weren't proof. Moments later, he was asleep, light and peaceful as a child.

Most of the town had followed Wheeler's example by the time the portly figure of Jase Elford rode back down main street after a bad tempered visit to Cal Underwood's log-built, comfortable ranch house.

Elford grinned at the memory of Underwood's indignation, turning his mount up one of the innumerable little side alleys that served for streets even in Santiago's American quarter.

Dawn was just beginning to colour the sky a pale rose, signalling another day of heat, as he pulled up outside the rear door of a whitewashed, spacious building, carelessly tied his mount and knocked sharply on the cool, sun-worn timber.

He must have been expected, because the door swung open immediately. Without ceremony, Elford shouldered his way inside and sauntered along the passageway to the neat sitting-room.

'Come in, why don't you,' his unwilling host snapped as Elford settled himself into a comfortable chair. Before he could answer, the other went on, 'And I thought we agreed you were never to come here. You know if anyone sees you with me, we're finished!'

'Relax,' Elford ordered, waving an airy hand. 'Things have changed. You might want to sit down 'cause you ain't gonna like any part o' what I got to tell you . . .'

For upwards of a minute, the big man spoke quietly, while his companion listened without comment.

'So you can see how it is now,' Elford finished. He shook his head in admiration. 'I allus wondered how you got that yella bastard Underwood to come in with us,' he admitted, shaking his head in admiration, 'But now I can . . .'

'I told you that!' the other interrupted, 'He murdered a pimp back East and I—'

'Yeah,' Elwood agreed, breaking in in turn, 'But now I know just why you happened to be there. It needn't make too much difference,' he went on blandly, 'but we ain't goin' no equal shares no more.'

'We can talk about that later,' his companion shrugged indifferently. 'But how did you find out about me and Cal?'

'I seen his girl,' Elford leered. 'Knew who she was straight off and after I put two an' two together, it naturally come up four.'

Without replying, his companion rose and stretched languidly, before suggesting, 'How about a drink, to seal our new partnership?'

'Sure, anything you say . . . partner,' Elford leered.

CHAPTER FIVE

Wheeler wasn't sure whether it was the sunlight or the shouting which dragged him from the bed and sent him staggering to the window, pistol in hand.

What he saw through the glass, though, drove the last vestiges of sleep from his brain. Swiftly, he scrambled into trousers, shirt and gunbelt. Ignoring his cane, he snatched up coat and hat, barged through the door and leapt down the stairs two at a time.

The scene hadn't changed much from the view he'd had from the window of the hotel room, as he emerged into the street.

Late morning sunlight, shame-faced men holding guns, and the still, pathetic figure of Lou Underwood, hands tied behind his back, standing on the rough, flat boards of a wagon, while the noose around his neck snaked upwards into the darkness of the livery barn.

And in the centre of it all, hair golden in the sunlight, Delia Underwood flourished a shotgun and dared her brothers' accusers to try something.

'There ain't gonna be no lynchin' here, Tyson,' she was snapping through gritted teeth at the fat,

41

soft-looking man wearing a fast draw gunbelt and the star of a town marshal.

'You're right, Miz Delia,' the man shot back with a bark of laughter. 'This here is legal execution of sentence from a duly constituted court.'

Silence, watchful and intense, fell upon the crowd as the girl digested this. Her eyes were star bright as she whispered, 'I don't believe it! You got that horrible old drunk to convict Lou,' she went on, jerking a firm little chin in the direction of a dishevelled old man who leaned blearily against the wall of the hotel. 'He never had a chance!'

'He had as much chance as he's gonna—' the marshal began, then he stopped abruptly, listening to a thin tune suddenly floating on the sunlit air. Someone, somewhere was whistling 'Shenendoah.'

'I ain't sure about your legal precedent, Marshal,' began the voice of Cord Wheeler, as he shouldered his way, polite but firm, through a crowd that shrank anxiously away from him on both sides.

'But as Mr Underwood's legal representative,' he continued, 'I'm duly informin' you that, nowadays, it's illegal to hang anyone without givin' them the chance to appeal to a Federal court. And besides, I don't like lynchings, especially not before breakfast.' He touched his hat to the girl as he emerged into the clear space between her and the lawman, ignoring the glare she threw in his direction and went on mildly, 'So just cut 'im down . . . or I'll do it.' Without replying, the marshal jerked his head in Underwood's direction and a narrow-shouldered, grubby deputy, barely older than the girl himself, shambled forward to climb into the bed of the wagon.

'I'd admire for you to try, Mr Fancy Pants,' the deputy sneered, trying to sound hopeful and tough, but managing neither.

'Happy to!' Wheeler snapped and the Smith & Wesson was in his hand and spouting flame. The rope around Lou Underwood's neck parted with a crack and, as the deputy turned to gape, he felt his belt grasped by an iron hand which jerked him off the wagon bed, to fly through the air and crash into the nearby hitching rail. Blearily, the deputy raised on to an elbow, only to lapse into unconsciousness as Wheeler slammed the butt of his pistol into the side of the thin youngster's head.

'Now, about this ... um ... murder, Marshal,' Wheeler began, as he turned from the smashed hitching rail. 'Let's just get Mr Underwood in a cell, nice and safe, then I'll look at the body. After all,' he continued mildly, gesturing absently with a right hand full of revolver, 'we wouldn't want any more accidents ... would we?'

Marshal Tyson, however, was made of sterner stuff than at first appeared.

'Sentence has been passed,' he began officiously, 'And said sentence is gonna—'

'Who passed the sentence, Marshal?' Wheeler enquired mildly.

'Why, the judge, like allus,' Tyson sneered.

'And the good judge,' Wheeler continued remorselessly, 'has he got a licence to practise law in this state?'

'Licence?' Tyson gaped.

'Yeah, see, lawyer or judge got to have a Federal licence,' Wheeler explained. 'They ain't got one, none o' their decisions is legal. You hang a man based on his say so,' Wheeler finished, 'and he ain't got a licence to practise, well, it's murder, plain and simple.'

Briefly, he examined the aghast Tyson, before saying, 'Now, about that cell. And just who is he supposed to have murdered?'

Now it was Wheeler's turn for a shock, as Tyson said, 'Fella name o' Elford. Talk says you knew 'im.'

'Cause o' death was this here bullet hole in his chest, which any fool can see. Hole's big enough to drive a team through,' Tyson finished as he moved gratefully away from the body.

'Sure looks that way,' Wheeler admitted, as he stooped to smell the dead man's mouth and then examine the blued lips which had drawn away from the teeth in a sardonic grin. Behind him, Hooper Satz, the thin deputy whom Wheeler had used to demolish the hitching rail, gave a bray of laughter.

'Sure can't understand what he finds so funny,' Satz offered, 'But just look at him grin.'

'Yeah,' Wheeler agreed thoughtfully. 'He sure found something funny. Are those the clothes he was wearing?'

The undertaker, to whose shop the body had been brought, stepped out of the shadows and said diffidently, 'Yes, everything just as he came in.'

'Give me a hand, will you?' Wheeler beckoned to

the little man and together they managed to turn the naked body on its side.

For a moment, Wheeler scanned Elford's back, then he said, 'Marshal, take a look here, will you?'

Reluctantly, Tyson heaved his massive bulk across to the bench and looked down at the white expanse of flabby muscle.

'Don't see nothing,' he shrugged,

'No, there isn't anything to see, is there?' Wheeler confirmed mildly.

'What's your point, Mr Detective?' Tyson snapped. 'Make it plain so's us hicks can understand!'

'OK,' Wheeler said quietly. 'The point is: where did the bullet come out?'

'Where did . . . why. . . ?' Tyson gaped.

'And in case you don't know,' Wheeler went on, 'the point of that is that most every handgun you'll find in use on the range has got enough punch to throw a slug clean through a man at anything up to twenty feet.' He looked doubtful.

'Takes something unusual to leave the slug in the body. Derringer or one o' them li'l hideout Colts. Know anyone with a derringer around town, Marshal?' Wheeler finished.

'No,' Tyson said although Wheeler caught the flicker of hesitation behind the words. 'Are you about through here?'

'Nope,' Wheeler admitted, with a gentle head shake. 'I want to look at his clothes, then I want to see where you found the body.'

'It was a derringer, right enough,' Wheeler explained,

holding the grubby little lead pellet up to the light. 'Your undertaker's done a mite o' doctoring and he managed to get it out. Miz Delia, you don't need to stay for this,' he finished kindly.

For a moment, the white-faced girl glared at the detective, but something seemed to change her mind and she said politely, 'Thank you for your concern, but if it's to do with Lou, then I think I definitely need to be here.'

The day was drawing to a close and having completed his investigation, Wheeler had sauntered over to the marshal's office to compare notes. Delia Underwood had been collecting her brother's supper tray and had come into the office of the jail after hearing the sound of voices.

'We don't want no female here, faintin' and havin' the vapours—' Tyson began.

'Miz Underwood doesn't strike me as the faintin' type, Marshal,' Wheeler interrupted, as he ushered the girl to a vacant seat. 'And I'm sayin' she's got the right to be here.' he finished icily.

'Hell, it's her funeral,' Tyson shrugged. 'So you're figgering this here Elford fella was shot with a derringer. So what? They ain't that uncommon.'

'No,' Wheeler admitted, 'but it does mean we can clear up one point. Does your brother own one o' them little hideout guns, Miz Underwood?' he asked

'He doesn't even own a revolver, Mr Wheeler,' the girl said frankly. 'Pa hates short guns for some reason, won't have one in the house. He taught me and Lou to use a rifle and Lou ain't got nothing but his Winchester.'

'Then how come we found him by the body, a coupla minutes after the shooting, holding a Colt?' Tyson sneered. 'And it had been fired purty recent, too.'

'What did he say?' Wheeler asked.

'Says he found it lying by the body, if'n you can believe that,' Tyson said. 'Says he heard the shots and come a runnin' and the gun was just lyin' there.'

'Elford have a piece?' Wheeler asked.

'Nope,' Satz, the deputy said. 'But he was wearin' a gunbelt with an empty holster.' Wheeler sighed and rubbed a hand through his short brown hair.

'And nobody figgered that it might have been Elford's gun and the reason it had been fired was because he'd shot at whoever'd killed him?' he asked gently.

'Say, Marshal,' Satz began wonderingly, 'mebbe that's how it could have happened!'

Giving his deputy a glare, Tyson snapped, 'Yeah and mebbe Lou bought that gun without anyone knowing and kept it hid. Do you know this cattle dealer?' he demanded of the girl.

'He did some business with Pa,' she admitted reluctantly, before saying with a rush, 'I guess you might as well know, 'cause someone's bound to tell you. Last time Mr Elford was here he . . . well . . . he was . . . he insulted me and Lou threatened to kill him if he ever so much as looked at me agin.' For a moment a hand covered her downcast eyes, then she looked up through lashes bright with tears.

'Billy and some of the boys heard him, but I swear he wouldn't have done it!'

'Ain't that what you'd call a motive, Mr Fancy Pants Detective?' Tyson asked, with a sneer.

'Could be,' Wheeler answered mildly. 'You figger Lou knew Elford was in town?' he asked the girl.

'I don't know,' she admitted. 'He might have done but—'

'O' course, he did,' said Tyson. 'That grey Jase rode stood out like a poisoned thumb.'

'The grey had been in the livery barn all day and you seem to know a lot about a fella whom most people say was never in town before today, Marshal,' Wheeler offered softly.

'I . . . I . . . was askin' around, doin' my job,' Tyson blustered. 'Can't have folks like Mr Elford gettin' shot by range scum. He coulda brought a lot o' money into this town.'

'Sure,' Delia Underwood sneered, jerking up from her chair. 'Only we all know whose pocket most of that money would end up in, don't we, Marshal!'

'Why, you goddamn nester's brat,' Tyson exploded. 'I oughta—'

'Sit down, afore you say somethin' I might have to take exception to,' Wheeler interrupted. 'Miz Underwood's a lady and is to be treated like one, at all times and by everybody, 'cause if she ain't, someone's gonna get a lesson in manners. And on that, Marshal, you have my personal guarantee.' The mild tone and New Orleans courtliness did nothing to dispel the resolution behind the words, and Tyson, who knew a dangerous man when he saw one, subsided.

'But, whatever you say,' he began, mildly for him,

'we still found Lou holding a gun by the body. If he didn't shoot him, who did?'

'Well, see,' Wheeler began, 'that's what I was comin' to. It don't really matter if Lou did shoot him.'

'And why in hell's that?' Tyson demanded.

' 'Cause it weren't the shot that killed him,' was the reply.

CHAPTER SIX

For several moments, the office was still as death, its occupants riveted on the man who had just dropped his bombshell. Unconcerned, Wheeler scratched a match and touched it to the end of his cigar and, instantly, the spell was broken.

'How in hell d'you know he wasn't shot?' Tyson demanded.

'Coupla things,' said Wheeler. 'First off, there weren't enough blood. Only a smidgeon on his shirt and when I looked, not much more on the ground where you found him. I seen a lot of men shot,' Wheeler admitted, 'And there's always an awful lot o' blood, 'cause the heart just naturally pumps it out. Shoot a fella after his heart stops an' the blood stays in the body 'cause the heart ain't workin' to push it out.' Wheeler spread his hands. 'Simple.'

'Besides,' the man from El Paso went on, 'as soon as I saw that look on his face, I knew what killed him.'

'What?' demanded Hooper Satz.

'Strychnine.' Wheeler said shortly. 'That grin you saw on his face is called by the medicos the *risus sardonicus*,' he grinned. 'I ain't sure how you say it,

50

but I saw a man who died of it once and that's what Old Doc Parsons called it. It was him explained about the gunshot wounds, too. I used to work for him down South.' Wheeler felt under no obligation to add that Parsons had been the prison doctor there while Wheeler had been serving his sentence.

'And you're sure about this, Mr Wheeler?' Delia Underwood asked fiercely.

Before Wheeler could reply, Tyson intervened, 'Sure or not, you ain't got nothin' that'll stand in a court of law.'

'Not yet,' Wheeler admitted, 'but I sent a coupla samples from Elford's body off to a government man I know. He'll soon tell us if Elford died from strychnine.' It was a monumental bluff, but from the look on Tyson's face, one that was unlikely to be called. Still, the Marshal of Santiago was game.

'I can't release him just on this Wheeler's say-so,' he stated, forestalling the girl as she turned towards him and made to speak.

'He'll have to stay here until the circuit judge arrives. I'll telegraph for him today and he'll be here in a coupla weeks.'

'Guess that'll have to do,' the girl said. 'At least you won't have the death of another innocent man on your conscience, Marshal.'

'No,' Tyson muttered at her back as Wheeler courteously allowed her to precede him through the ramshackle, sun-warped door of the jail. 'I won't have it on my conscience. I'll leave that to Jase's boys, when they get here.'

Out in the dusty street, the sun was dipping past

the roofs of the houses on Santiago's main street as Delia Underwood squared her shoulders and turned to Wheeler.

'Mr Wheeler, I owe you an apology,' she blurted out. Before Wheeler could answer she gabbled on, 'When I saw you drinking with that O Bar O crowd, I thought you'd thrown in with them. They hate us and that Davy Wrawlings is just the meanest thing. I don't know what I ever saw in him, though Lisa says she thinks he's kinda cute, but I said . . .'

'Whoa, whoa, whoa.' Wheeler threw up his hands in protest. 'First off, I never throw in with anyone, 'less they ask me. An' Jesse and Davy look like they can look out for themselves and besides,' he finished reasonably, 'they sure struck me as square.'

'Square!' the girl exploded. 'They as good as accused my Pa of rustlin'!'

All in all, it was an uncharacteristically thoughtful Cord Wheeler who pushed through the door of Santiago's run-down general store.

'Lucifers,' Wheeler answered the owner's query, tendering a silver dollar. 'Don't seem run off'n your feet,' Wheeler offered mildly, pocketing both matches and change.

'You called that about right, friend,' came the disgusted reply and after the usual exchange of civilities the man behind the counter said, 'Sure a good thing you stopped that l'il fandango this morning!'

'Underwoods friends of yours?' Wheeler asked.

'Nope, I just hate a set up,' came the surprising reply.

'You figger it that way?' Wheeler asked.

'Let's just say it wouldn't be the first time,' the storekeeper responded.

'That fella Elford was pretty well known around town, I hear,' Wheeler suggested.

'Well, I ain't never seen him.' The man shrugged. 'Never bought so much as a sack o' smokin' here.'

Wheeler nodded absently, passing along the counter as he did so to a glass case containing a display of second-hand pistols. Scanning the weapons on offer, he asked absently, 'Sell many .41 centre-fire cartridges?'

'You mean the sort that fit a derringer?' the man asked, and when Wheeler nodded confirmation, he went on, 'Don't keep 'em at all. No one on this range got any use for a hideout gun.'

Wheeler had not been gone from the store for many minutes when its owner received a far more uncomfortable visitor. Billy Vargas, the Underwood *segundo*, with whom Wheeler had dealt on the first day, slouched up to the counter and demanded, 'That fancy pants. What'd he want?'

Wheeler, meanwhile, had called into the cantina, for a well-earned cup of coffee and some information.

Foot hooked on to the bar rail, he sipped the steaming liquid and listened while Willie the bartender and Sly Templeton discussed the events of the previous day.

'Tyson's a rattler,' Willie stated with uncharacteristic vehmence.

'Worse,' Templeton corrected. 'Rattler'll warn you

afore it strikes. Don't you expect nothin' like that from Tyson,' he finished eyeing Wheeler significantly.

'Oh, I don't like snakes,' Wheeler assured the old man, 'but I'm sure confused about the set up around here. I've met Jesse Wrawlings and his boy Davy and I figure they're straight. But then Miz Delia tells me they accused her pa o' rustling, which she claims is a downright lie. What's goin' on down here?'

Templeton studied the younger man for several seconds, before saying, 'Let's you and me sit down and mebbe I can set you straight.'

'Cal Underwood come out to this part of the country just after the war, from back East,' Templeton began, his tones harking back to old Virginia. 'His wife died on the way and he was left with Miz Delia and Lou, both of 'em barely walkin'. It's an old story,' Templeton went on. 'He fought Comanche, rustlers, jayhawkers, all the scum of the West an' about five years ago, he had one of the best ranches in the South West and the best crew, men who'd ridden for him for years. I know, because I was one of them for more years . . . anyhow, one day . . . I ain't sure . . . but seems like he just went crazy. Fired the crew and brought in a lot of bar sweepings, who knew more about guns than they did about cows. Jesse Wrawlings, him and ol' Cal bein' good friends, mebbe states his feelin's about the new men too plain and him an' Cal ain't spoke since.

'Jed Taylor, Wrawling's *segundo*, used to be foreman.' Templeton continued. 'Him and old Cal was close as brothers and even he don't know what happened. Or if he does,' the old man finished shrewdly, 'he ain't saying.'

'And Underwood's old crew, what happened to them?' Wheeler asked.

'Most of them drifted, 'cept me.' The old man shrugged and grinned shamefacedly. 'Bust my leg coupla year before. It don't bother me too much but it won't let me sit a horse for cow work, so I clean up this place fer Willie. I got lucky, too. Miz Keely was just startin' her hotel about then and I got a job helpin' out around the place.'

'So Miz Keely arrived in town about the time old man Underwood made all these changes to his ranch?' Wheeler asked softly.

'I couldn't say for sure,' Templeton admitted, 'but it must've been about then, otherwise how'd I've got the job?' he explained, with unassailable logic.

'Sure sounds like it, don't it?' Wheeler admitted, before asking, 'What brand does Underwood use?'

'Brands Bar U, like this,' the old man explained, drawing a U with a bar projecting backwards from its left upright.

'And afore you ask,' the old man went on, 'Wrawlings' O Bar O looks like this.' Carefully, Templeton drew two neat circles joined across the top with a straight bar.

For a moment, Wheeler studied the old man's drawings before asking, 'Any other big ranches claim to be losing cows?'

'Dunno about losing stock,' Templeton admitted, with a shrug, 'but there are a coupla big outfits to the west. Biggest is probably the Flyin' B.' He drew a neat

B with a straight bar flowing back from the top left. 'They brand like this.'

Wheeler nodded and asked 'What's the other outfit?'

'Circle R,' Templeton stated, drawing a small O followed by an R twice its size. 'Baxter, their manager, figured to get cute, so they changed the brand and use stamping irons. All the other spreads just run the brands anyhow.'

'Any cow thief lighted in this part o' the world would think he'd died and gone to heaven,' Wheeler offered.

'Sure.' Sly Templeton nodded his agreement. 'Running irons and the Mex border sure make a temptin' combination.'

'Let me just see if I got these brands straight, Sly,' Wheeler asked, drawing swiftly on an old envelope. He tendered the result to the old man.

On the paper had been drawn :

$$O^-O \quad ^-U \quad ^-B \quad ^OR$$

'O' course, the next question is: who could steal from who?' Wheeler began, after the old man had examined the paper and pronounced it correct.

'That's easy,' Templeton interrupted. 'Wrawlings could steal from the Bar U and the Flyin' B could blot the Bar U easy enough. Except both them ranches is run by honest men. The only ranch whose crew is a nest o' crooks couldn't steal from anyone. At least,' he added shrewdly, 'not using Cal Underwood's' brand.'

'What about Elford?' Wheeler asked quietly.

'It ain't generally known,' Templeton admitted, 'but his registered brand is B H B, I see that on a contract ol' Cal had one time. Never seen the mark on a cow, though,' he finished.

Wheeler added the brand beneath each of the others and tendered the end result to Templeton:

On the paper now was drawn:

$$O^-O \qquad ^-U \qquad ^-B \qquad ^OR$$

$$BHB \qquad BHB \qquad BHB \qquad BHB$$

Wearily, the old man scratched his frowzy head.

'Blamed if I can see it,' he admitted. 'The two fellas that you'd figger most likely to be the culprits can't blot their brands so's they can steal from anyone else. What you figger to do now?'

'Nothin' I can do,' Wheeler shrugged, 'except wait.'

Abruptly from the street, there came the sound of hoofs. Templeton eased himself out of his chair and sauntered over to the batwings.

'You may find some entertainment while you're waitin',' he offered over his shoulder. 'I ain't sure,' he went on, pointing across the street, as Wheeler limped up to join him, 'but unless I miss my guess, that's Elford's crew and they sure don't look like they come fer no Sunday-school picnic.'

'Sure don't,' Wheeler agreed mildly, shouldering his way through the batwings.

'Where you goin' now?' Templeton demanded.

His answer came drifting back on the dust-scented breeze. Somebody, somewhere was whistling 'Shenendoah'.

CHAPTER SEVEN

By the time Wheeler had crossed the street, the B H B riders had dispersed to care for their mounts.

Only one horse remained, tied negligently to the hitching rail and Wheeler passed deliberately on the near side, so as to obtain a clear look at Elford's brand. What he saw stamped on the pony's flank momentarily riveted his glance, but with an effort he tore his eyes away and continued his shambling progress as though nothing untoward had occurred.

Outwardly calm, Wheeler's mind was racing. Sure, Elford branded B H B. Only in common with many in the grass country, he contracted his brand to make fewer strokes for the iron man. What appeared on the flank of the horse was B-B and suddenly Elford didn't look quite so innocent.

Quietly entering the office, with his mind doing swift geometry on the brands Templeton had previously described, Wheeler found himself confronted by the unsavoury sight of Tyson slumped in his chair, while across from him was a second man who was snarling, 'I don't like it, Waldo. Whoever got Jase had to know somethin'.'

Abruptly, as Wheeler pushed the door shut behind

him, Tyson motioned with his hand, a cutting-off gesture across his throat which brought the other out of his chair, turning as he did so to confront the man from El Paso.

Wheeler's first impression of Elford's right-hand man was of an immense, hairy bulk from which gleamed two piggy eyes above a cigar thrust somehow into the tangle of beard.

Abruptly, the cigar was hurled away and the giant demanded, 'And who in hell might you be?'

Carefully, Wheeler transferred the brass knob of his cane to his left hand. He leaned on it gratefully, casually hooking his right thumb into the broad gunbelt next to the holstered Smith & Wesson. The green eyes under the wide brimmed Texas hat were icy although the voice was mildly courteous as he said, 'I might be Santa Claus and you might have decent manners, although I'm bound to say, the one is as unlikely as the other.'

For a second the giant digested this. Then, with a roar of rage he lurched forward, only to find himself barred by the marshal. A few whispered words and then Tyson was turning to Wheeler, with the giant apparently mollified.

'No call for anyone to go losin' their wool,' he began smoothly. 'Mr Wheeler, this here's Abe Vargas, the late Mr Elford's ramrod. You've mebbe met his brother, Billy. Works for Cal Underwood.'

'Yeah,' Wheeler said slowly, 'although last time I saw him he was branching out into the porterin' business. Wanted to charge me five dollars to carry my bag,' he finished mildly.

The giant laughed appreciatively. 'Punk kid,' he rumbled, without heat, before asking maliciously, 'I hope he never roughed you up too much, dude.'

'Nope,' Wheeler answered coldly. 'I needed some exercise, though next time you see him you might ask him how his jaw is.' Pointedly, Wheeler dusted off his boot before adding, 'He didn't look too healthy last time I saw him.'

Another explosion seemed imminent but, all at once Vargas appeared to think better of it. Instead, he slouched past Wheeler to the door. Pausing with his hand on the brass knob, he glared at the other over his shoulder.

'Best watch your step, dude. Not all the family are as easy as l'il Billy.' Then he was gone with the door slammed behind him.

'Nice fella,' Wheeler offered as he limped across to the marshal's desk.

'You better watch out,' Tyson sneered, ' 'Cause he's right. You wouldn't find Abe as easy to handle as young Billy.'

Wheeler nodded absently and then asked inconsequentially, 'What's Elford's brand?'

'B H B,' Tyson said without thought. 'I mean, I think so . . . could ask around but I think that's his mark. You got any idea about his killer?' the marshal finished artlessly.

'Nope,' Wheeler shrugged, not daring to look at the man for fear that his thoughts might show on his face. Tyson suddenly seemed to know a hell of a lot about the business of a man he professed not to have met before.

*

'So what d'you think?' Wheeler demanded.

'Strikes me you're right,' Sly Templeton admitted quietly, tipping his chair in order to re-examine Wheeler's drawing by the light of one of the cantina's flaring oil lamps.

On a new scrap of paper was now drawn :

$$\bar{\ }U \qquad O\bar{\ }O \qquad \bar{\ }B \qquad {}^{O}R$$

$$B\bar{\ }B \qquad B\bar{\ }B \qquad B\bar{\ }B \qquad B\bar{\ }B$$

'It'd be purty easy,' Templeton assured Wheeler. 'Join the top of the U and add a B and an O, takes care of Underwood's brand. Coupla Os on the bottom of O Bar O makes that B H B. The Flyin' B adds another B and Circle R joins the bottom of the R and adds a bar and a small O. I figger that gives you your master brand, 'cause Elford could have stole cows from all of 'em. Question is, what you gonna do now?'

'Just perzactly nuthin',' Wheeler shrugged. 'Just 'cause they can do it don't mean they are. Any half smart lawyer'd have it laughed out of court. Elford, or rather,' he corrected himself, 'his heirs'd put their hands up and say: "My, My, what a coincidence", and there ain't one blasted thing to say otherwise.'

'No,' Wheeler went on, 'these *hombres* are clever. You need to find cows with the brands still raw, or something like, 'cause once them brands are healed and the dogies are on the trail, ain't no one can say they ain't legitimate B H B stock.' He shook his head admiringly. 'And that,' he finished, 'is the real beauty of it.'

It wasn't, however, the beauty of their scheme that sent Tyson banging on the rear door of a certain whitewashed building in the better part of town, in the early part of the evening.

Darkness had barely fallen and, as he expected, his welcome was less then cordial.

'What in hell are you doin' here?' his host demanded instantly as Tyson shouldered his way inside.

'We got trouble, boss . . .' the fat man began nervously.

'For Christ's sake, shut up,' the other snapped venomously. 'Someone'll hear you. Goddammit . . .' The effort at control was monumental but it was made and then Tyson's boss was saying, 'Get in there.'

Once safely ensconced in the side room, Tyson blurted, 'It's that goddamn detective! He's been askin' a lot of questions about Jase's brand and sich. And he knows Jase was poisoned afore he was shot and' – he paused significantly – 'he knows what he was shot with. Asked ol' Rafe down to the store if he ever sold them sort of cartridges.'

If anything Tyson said had significance to his companion, it didn't show. After a moment's thought, the other said, 'Let 'im look. He's got nothin'.'

'S'pose he figgers out the brand business!' Tyson

bleated. 'I think Jase was wrong about him. He ain't no fancy pants hired gun, he's smart and he's tricky. I sure wish Jase had figgered on using someone else to deal with Old Cal.'

'Don't worry about Cal or Wheeler,' the other sneered, 'I've got an idea that'll solve both those little problems for us. Get hold of Abe and tell 'im . . .'

'Smart,' Tyson admitted as he was unceremoniously pushed through the back door some time later, when full dark had descended. 'Smart and tricky as a rattler,' he nodded, with a self-satisfied smile. 'Let's see you get out of this one, Mr Fancy Pants.'

'Cord, you better get out here,' Jesse Wrawlings offered as he started through the batwings at a run, 'Looks like Vargas and his brother are fixing to hang that boy.'

Wheeler had been in the cantina, having a last cup of coffee, while vaguely toying with the idea of going to bed, but Wrawlings' words catapulted him out of the chair and through the still swinging doors.

The scene in the street left no room for doubt. As he swung up the centre of the main drag, he could see a mob of angry men standing in front of the jail, several with ropes. At the front was the tall figure of Abe Vargas, flanked by his brother. The B H B foreman was hammering words at Tyson, pinning him to the spot.

'An' I say we ain't waitin' fer no circuit judge,' the big man snapped. 'Don't need one. That fella's as guilty as hell and you know it!'

'My, you're an awful pushing kind of a fella, ain't you, Mr Vargas?' said a mild, cultured voice from the back of the crowd, before Tyson could answer his tormentor. Then Cord Wheeler was stumping on to the front porch of the jail, followed by the giant form of Jesse Wrawlings.

'Marshal,' the man from El Paso began, 'I'm gittin' awful tired o' doin' your job for you. So I'm just gonna say this: guilty or not, anything happens to that boy before he comes to trial, I'll hunt down and kill every last man involved. You have my personal guarantee upon that.' He paused before adding, 'Whoever they are.'

'There's room enough for two on that cotton-wood,' Abe Vargas began, then he stopped because Wheeler had flipped back the left side of his coat, exposing the old bone-handled Smith & Wesson in its stiff, greasy holster.

'That's surely true,' Wheeler stated flatly, 'but before it happens there's gonna be some nice fresh graves up in Boot Hill and you and six, seven of your boys are gonna have no further interest in the matter.' Magically, Vargas found himself looking down the bore of Wheeler's pistol as the detective finished coldly, 'Now, you and these others just get on back to your hog wallow, and don't come back agin 'til trial day.'

Angrily, Vargas motioned his men away from the porch of the jailhouse. They went, although not without some angry muttering and for a moment, Vargas paused, glaring furiously at the man who had bested him.

'You know this ain't over, Mr Fancy Pants El Paso detective,' he snarled, massive hands flexing in a paroxysm of rage. 'You know that . . . don't you?' he finished in a whisper aching with hate.

Wheeler smiled, a small, grim tightening of the lips. Then his pistol whirled, to finish nestling back in the worn holster.

'You'd be a considerable disappointment to me, Mr Vargas,' he began, 'if you didn't include vindictiveness amongst your other vices. Of course,' Wheeler went on mildly, deliberately clasping his hands behind his back, 'If you feel lucky . . .'

For an achingly long moment, tension was a living, breathing thing in the dirty little street, then Vargas sneered, 'You'll keep. There'll be better times,' he finished, as he turned and stomped away.

'I wouldn't turn your back on that one, Mr Wheeler,' Sly Templeton offered, as he stepped out of the shadows, slipping his old .44 Remington away as he did so.

'No,' Wheeler acknowledged, 'I do believe that'd be sound advice. Although,' he added quietly, for no ears but his own, 'I'd sure like to know how the son of a gun knew I was a detective from El Paso.'

CHAPTER EIGHT

'Marshal,' Wheeler began whimsically, as the would-be lynching party faded into the bright lights of the cantina, followed closely by its erstwhile leader, 'I believe you've just hired yourself a new deputy.'

'County don't pay me enough fer the one I got as it is. Can't afford no more,' Tyson stated pompously.

'Oh, that won't matter,' Wheeler assured him. 'I'll be glad to do it just to help out. And in case you was wondering, Marshal,' Wheeler finished icily, 'I ain't askin you, I'm tellin' you.'

'Phew,' Wheeler offered as he kicked shut the door of the office and dumped his battered carpet bag on the desk, 'don't you boys believe in the benefits of fresh air?'

'Too much fresh air can be bad for a fella,' Hooper Satz offered.

'And just how would that be?' Wheeler asked unwisely, busy with the contents of his bag.

'If'n he gets too much let into hisself through bullet holes,' Satz crowed, slapping a leg in appreciation of his own joke.

Wheeler joined in the laugh at his expense.

'On account of not intending to be subject to any such ventilation,' he said, lifting out a package tightly wrapped in oilskin, 'I brought along a l'il equalizer.' For a couple of minutes Wheeler busied himself with his unwrapping, then he straightened and in his hands was a wicked-looking shotgun, its twin barrels barely a foot long and the butt shaped into a neat brass-shod pistol grip.

'I'm betting that ain't much use over long range,' Tyson sneered, nervous despite himself.

'Nope,' Wheeler admitted, with a cheerful wink at a riveted Hooper Satz. 'But it'll clear anything in front of it across a barroom. I ain't aiming to get outnumbered,' he finished significantly, as he thumbed in two giant cartridges and snapped the weapon closed.

'Hsst, hsssst, Miz Delia. Oh Miz Delia.' The call was barely loud enough to carry across the sidewalk, but it stopped Delia Underwood in her tracks. She slipped her brother's supper tray under one arm and advanced cautiously through the well-tracked dust in front of Rafe Pardoe's run-down general store. Moving forward, she could just make out the lighter area of darkness between the two buildings. Abruptly she stopped. Someone was crouched against the near wall. Cautiously, the girl advanced until moonlight lit the features of the waiting figure and the girl gave a cry of relief.

'Miz Keely!'

'Ssh, fer Chri— I mean, not so loud, dear!' the

68

figure responded urgently. 'I want to help you get your brother out of that awful jail. Listen,' she began urgently, 'take this. . . .'

The door of the office was opened almost immediately in answer to Delia Underwood's hesitant knock. It was Hooper Satz with his hand on the door handle and at sight of her, his homely, broken-toothed mouth split in a friendly grin.

'Come right in, Miz Underwood,' he offered, holding wide the door and standing back. 'You're lookin' right purty tonight, ma'am,' he offered politely.

Despite her nervousness, the girl managed a tight smile as she walked across to the iron-bound door that led to the back of the jail. Satz moved in front of her quickly, opening the door and politely ushering her through. She offered Wheeler a spare smile while ignoring Tyson, whose face was set in a leer of lascivious speculation.

'Now there,' he began, following the girl's shapely form as she slipped through the door, 'is something I'd—' Then he stopped, because the look on Wheeler's face as the detective examined him said more than any torrent of abuse or threats could ever have.

Once Satz had left, Delia Underwood wasted no time. Despite her brother's protests at what was being done to his dinner, she plunged her hand into the big slab of apple pie. What she held when her fingers came out, drove all thought of food from the boy's mind.

'Where in hell did you get that?' he demanded.

'Never mind that!' the girl snapped. 'Just listen! When I go out, you count to fifty, then . . .'

'Marshal, I'm worried about Lou—' she said, but whatever Delia Underwood had planned to say was lost in the piercing screams that suddenly echoed from the back room of the jail.

Cursing fluently under his breath, Satz unbolted the door and pushed roughly through the opening. Silence followed, dragging, leaden-footed silence before the deputy reappeared. But it was a very sick-looking Hooper Satz and the reason for his slightly greenish tinge was soon apparent, as Lou Underwood pushed Satz out of the door in front of him and said in a voice he was plainly having trouble holding steady, 'Get Tyson's guns, D.'

In an instant, the girl had obeyed, slipping past her brother to throw the marshal's guns in the cell and lock the door on them. Without waiting for her brother to speak, she snapped impatiently, 'I expect you'll want to use that horse out front!'

Trying to pretend a resolution he was plainly a long way from feeling, Underwood said, 'Yeah, that's right. And don't try to stop me, Sis.

'Don't you try nothin' either, Tyson,' he went on shakily, twisting the petrified deputy to show the man's own gun in his back, 'or I'll let Hooper have it right here.'

Wheeler had been an interested, if amused, specta-tor to the Underwoods' idea of a jail break, but at mention of the horse, he stepped silently to the window.

70

For a moment, he scanned the street, before saying softly, 'Was I you, I think I'd leave that pony out front. Could be better if'n you go out the back way. Though, o'course, the fact is it'd be better if you just passed me the deputy's gun and went back to that nice comfortable bunk. You run and there ain't gonna be no one around to watch your back,' the detective finished significantly.

Caught in a welter of indecision, Underwood and the girl exchanged dubious glances. Then, the boy's chin stiffened.

'Thank you just the same, Mr Wheeler,' he said courteously, 'but I'd sooner take my chance with the wolves out there than this mangy excuse for a pack rat.' He nodded in Tyson's direction.

'Just git along, Hooper,' the boy continued, 'and don't do nothin' that'll make me have to kill you. Sis, just open that door. And stay in here outa the way,' he finished, as the girl made to precede him through the opening.

Reluctantly, she drew back and Underwood began to push Satz through the door.

Seeing his chance, with all eyes apparently intent on the prisoner, Tyson opened his mouth, ready to bellow a warning.

But Wheeler had caught the fat man's movement out the corner of his eye and he swivelled smoothly, drawing his pistol and laying it along the side of Tyson's head with clinical precision.

The fat man dropped like a stone and Wheeler swung back to the group in the doorway who were transfixed by the speed of events. His pistol twitched negligently as he said, 'Now, I really think you better get back in that cell!'

Delia Underwood opened her mouth to speak, but the objection, when it came, was from a surprising quarter.

'That ain't what I'd call a good idea,' Hooper Satz offered. 'Tyson ain't the fergivin' sort and we sure can't hold this jail if them B H B gunslingers come huntin' trouble. And you can bet, once they've had enough liquor, that's just what they're gonna do!'

Seeing the questioning look on the girl's face, he went on shame-facedly, 'I don't like the way Lou got railroaded, Miz Delia, but by myself, well . . . I couldn't do nothing!'

'I figger you've called it about right, Deputy,' Wheeler interrupted before the girl could answer. 'What'd you figger to do, Miz Delia, after you busted this knothead out?'

'We both know the mountains fairly well,' she said, shrugging, 'so I intended to just get lost, at least until that judge turned up. I told Lou where I've got the horses and supplies cached outside of town and a friend said she . . . I mean, they said they'd help me, when we needed more.'

'Sounds about the best we can do, given the set up,' Wheeler began, shaking his head doubtfully, 'But we still got to get him outta town.' After a moment, he went on, 'Deputy, if you're aimin' to help, douse that light.'

Almost instantly, the lamp flickered out and in the warm, dust-scented darkness, Wheeler's voice was saying quietly, 'Now, Mr Underwood, you just walk out the door, fork that pony and ride out of town. Just go nice and easy and if it comes to shootin', make sure you . . . miss!'

Given the lack of time and organization, it wasn't a bad plan and it really should have worked. Except Lou Underwood lifted his face as he rode past a pair of B H B hands who hadn't taken on enough bottled lightning to impair their eyesight, and to make matters worse, the moon chose just that moment to come scudding out innocently from behind a cloud.

Recognition was instant and mutual and, as Lou clapped spurs into his pony, Wheeler saw the cowboys reach for their weapons.

Without some intervention, Underwood would be shot down like a dog so, without hesitation, Wheeler jerked up his wicked little scatter gun.

Only it wasn't the men he aimed at but rather the solid wooden livery notice that swung above their heads.

Before either man could fire, Wheeler triggered both barrels. Caught by a blast of buckshot, the frayed, sun-dried rope supporting the outer edge of the sign parted like cotton and the heavy board swung down, catching the nearest man squarely in the side of the head and throwing him violently against his companion, whose first shot was triggered harmlessly into the air.

Both men were knocked sprawling on to the rough planks of the sidewalk. The first, hit by the sign, lay where he had fallen but the second man made to rise, only to slump back as the brass shod butt of Wheeler's shotgun crashed into the side of his head.

Without waiting to check on the condition of either man, Wheeler propped his empty shotgun on a convenient plank of the sidewalk, before stooping and grabbing up both men's guns.

'*Whew*,' he screamed, emptying both pistols as fast as he could in the direction of the moon. 'Get out here, you waddies, prisoner's gettin' away!'

Discarding the empty pistols, Wheeler swept up his shotgun and by the time the first of the B H B men were out in the street, he was past the jail and waving his pistol in the opposite direction to that taken by the fleeing Lou Underwood, while a grinning Hooper Satz fired his battered revolver at a perfectly innocent tin can squatting in the middle of the dusty street. It should perhaps go on record that the tin can suffered not the slightest damage consequent upon the broken-toothed one's ministrations.

'Get your horses, boys,' Wheeler ordered enthusiastically, 'He ain't got more'n five minutes start! Don't you forget now, Marshal wants him alive!' It was with difficulty that he hid his grin as the entire B H B contingent, having collected their mounts, headed out of town at a dead run . . . in precisely the wrong direction.

Feeling well satisfied with himself, Wheeler followed a grinning Hooper Satz back towards the jail, passing, as he did so, a little group who had gathered on the sidewalk to enjoy the excitement. Delia Underwood was there, standing next to Mariah Keely, the latter's hair covered with an elegant, light coloured mantilla. Framed together by some trick of the moonlight, Wheeler caught the profiles of the two women side on and what he saw there made him pause and look again.

'I wonder . . .' he began, then turned abruptly and limped off towards the telegraph office. If Ira didn't know, he could sure as hell find someone who did.

CHAPTER NINE

'Sly,' Wheeler began, pulling on the borrowed chaps, 'I wouldn't want it generally known that I ain't quite the greenhorn I may look. Could be useful later. Understand me?'

'Sure,' the older man grinned an acknowledgement, adding unwisely, 'I'm dumb.'

'I know it,' Wheeler returned with a grin, ' but I'm sure somethin' can be done with you, given time and patience.'

The B H B contingent had returned in ones and twos as the effect of the hard riding and whiskey made itself felt but not before Hooper Satz had aroused his esteemed boss by the simple expedient of pouring a bucket of water over his head. Satz had previously used the contents of the bucket to mop out the jail so, not unexpectedly, he found himself on the wrong end of Tyson's bad temper. Wheeler had left Tyson trying to round up a posse in the rose pink light of dawn and gone in search of Sly Templeton to borrow the equipment he needed to accompany the group.

'If'n there's one thing I can't stand,' Templeton grumbled, as Wheeler stood and shook the stiff leather into a more comfortable position, 'It's a smart-alec kid. S'pose you want a rifle, too?'

'Nope,' Wheeler stated, 'I want a carbine if'n you got one. I can hit most things at four hundred with a saddle gun and them long barrelled Winchesters are awkward if'n you're movin' through brush.'

'Particular, ain't you?' Templeton snapped, collecting a well-kept Winchester carbine from the rack in the tack room.

'This is mine,' he went on, before Wheeler could answer, 'An' I want it back clean an' in one piece!'

'Sure, sure, I ain't gonna hurt your museum relic,' came the flippant answer, but Templeton was hard put to supress a smile of satisfaction as he noted the thorough, methodical check Wheeler gave the weapon before sliding it carefully into its soft leather saddle boot. Glaring across at his companion, Wheeler demanded, 'Now, you got anything fit for a man to ride?'

Wheeler found Tyson and his men waiting in front of the jail. As he rode the little pinto he had chosen towards them, Ferris 'Rat' Oldman, let out a crow of laughter and demanded of the crowd, 'Well, lookee here, you comin' along to play at being a cowboy, dude?'

For a moment, their glances locked before Oldman's slid away and Wheeler said icily, 'Glad to see you got all the choya spines out o' your arse, Rat. Better be careful you don't pick up nothin' worse.' Without waiting for a reply, Wheeler glanced at Tyson and said, 'You deputizing all this scum or just your own particular rats?'

'These men are duly appointed officers, selected by me personally and—' Tyson began.

'Save it,' Wheeler interrupted frostily. 'You better just remember what I said. That boy comes back alive or someone'll answer to me. Are we leaving?'

Tyson shook his head. 'I got a few things to settle with the judge, warrants and such,' he admitted, 'but I want you boys back here, mounted and ready to go in 'bout an hour.'

Amidst half-hearted muttering, as well as a few black looks thrown in Wheeler's direction, the prospective posse men dispersed, leaving Wheeler to turn his pony in the direction of the sidewalk. Cowboy-like, he rode the few yards to find himself looking down at a big, craggy-faced man, in worn range clothes, who reached up a long-fingered hand and said, 'Mr Wheeler? I believe I am in your debt, suh. My name is Cal Underwood and I think I owe you the life of my son.'

The detective's eyes widened momentarily as he caught the familiar singing vowels of his home city.

'Come West before the war,' Underwood explained, after he and Wheeler had ensconced themselves in the cantina, with a pot of steaming coffee between them. 'Wife died birthin' Lou and Delia, so I just kept goin'. When I got here, seemed like the right place,' he finished simply.

'Sly Templeton said he thought you'd come from quite a long ways east, Missouri or mebbe even Louisiana, *n'est-ce pas?*' Wheeler asked innocently.

'*Non, je ne . . .*' Underwood responded before he could stop himself, 'I mean . . . I—'

'You mean you're from New Orleans,' Wheeler interrupted softly, 'raised on the bayous, like me. More than that,' he went on, examining the snapping brown eyes under the still black eyebrows, 'you're a Cajun.'

Before he could continue, Underwood jumped to his feet.

'I'm aware, suh,' he snapped, 'that I and my family owe you a debt that we'll be hard put to repay, but that doesn't give you leave to interfere in what is old and, might I add, very private business.' Abruptly he stopped and placed a hand on the table between them, while he ran the other shakily through his thinning grey hair.

'For God's sake,' the old man whispered, 'let the ghosts stay buried!' Wheeler could only watch as Underwood turned and blundered from the cantina into the burning sunlight of the street. Then he rose, let out a long breath and said, to no one in particular, 'Ol' Ira is sure gonna be a busy boy! And ain't Mollie gonna give me hell!'

The posse had been riding east for most of the day, following a plain trail, although Wheeler, who had seen and memorized the tracks Lou Underwood had left, knew perfectly well that the prints they were following hadn't been left by Tyson's prisoner, when Abe Vargas, who was in the lead, raised a meaty hand.

'These tracks are gettin' mighty fresh, boys,' the giant B H B foreman rumbled to the crowd in general. 'Can't be more'n an hour or two in front. Chet here,' he went on, encouraged by several curses of agreement, 'knows this country purty well and he says there's a little draw up ahead that's a good place to camp. How'll we play it, Marshal?' Vargas finished unexpectedly.

'We'll leave the horses here,' Tyson decided, 'and move up on foot. Mr Wheeler, you stay here with Mason and Sherwell,' he ordered spitefully, indicating two unsavoury-looking B H B men.

'Them ain't Lou's tracks!' Satz whispered vehemently, as he and Wheeler stripped riding gear from their mounts. 'And them we bin followin're at least two months old!'

'I'm pleased to see your eddication ain't bin neglected, at least in some areas,' Wheeler responded gravely. 'I bin a mite worried . . .'

'Quit joshin',' Satz snapped. 'I figger this is just a plan to leave you alone with them B H B scum so you can have a little accident! What in hell you gonna do? You want me to lose the posse and double back here, kinda watch your back?'

For a moment, the cold green eyes in the hard face softened and its contours broke into a rare smile as Wheeler dropped a hand lightly on to the other's shoulder.

'You're a good kid, and you're sure due to be some sort of a man one day, but I figger,' he went on, smile broadening, 'that they may be better shots than that tomato can back in town.'

'Oh,' Satz began, 'I told you my sights was off an'—'

'Yeah, you told me,' Wheeler interrupted, 'but I got another job for you. I can match any play these B H B waddies make but I need you to watch Vargas and the marshal. Can't have 'em hornin' in and makin' a gun play when I ain't lookin'. *Sabe?*'

'Sure,' the boy nodded, 'but—'

'No buts,' Wheeler interrupted, 'get your rifle. Looks like they're leaving.'

The posse had been gone a bare half hour and Wheeler had settled himself comfortably against a convenient tree root, when the short hairs on the back of his neck began to prickle. Obedient to the familiar signal, he rolled abruptly away from his back rest, coming smoothly to his feet, only to freeze with his hand halfway to his weapon as first Mason, then his partner, stepped from the shelter of the brush surrounding the camp, their rifles trained on Wheeler. Wheeler stood still. At twenty yards, a Winchester made a good argument.

'Been huntin' boys?' the detective asked innocently, at the same time clasping his hands loosely behind his back and eyeing the dwindling range as Mason moved towards him.

'Naw, we got what we come for, dude,' Mason rasped. 'Put up your hands.'

'Sure,' Wheeler responded mildly, raising both hands to shoulder height, as Mason lowered his weapon with a vicious grin, 'only . . .' he went on, before suddenly appearing to stumble forward.

As Mason turned, trying to bring up his rifle, Wheeler's right hand jerked, there was a flicker of light between the two men, and suddenly the ivory hilt of a throwing knife was growing out of the B H B man's throat.

For one fatal second, Sherwell gaped at the sight of his partner, and in that instant, Wheeler's stumble had turned into a neat shoulder roll, bringing the detective to his feet just beyond Mason's body, with the Smith & Wesson roaring in his hand as he straightened.

His first shot caught the second cowboy high in the chest, knocking him backwards into the dirt. Spitting curses, Sherwell threw aside the rifle and dropped a hand to his holstered Colt, only to jerk backwards as Wheeler's second shot sliced into his forehead, depositing his Stetson and a goodish portion of his brains into the dirt.

Swiftly, Wheeler scanned the clearing and surrounding brush, until, sure that Vargas hadn't sent back a spare man to cover all bets, he moved carefully to Mason and jerked the wicked little blade out of his throat.

Without a glance at either man, Wheeler turned to the horses. Swiftly, he saddled the pinto, stuffing Sly Templeton's capacious saddlebags with food and a liberal supply of cartridges for the Winchester. For a moment, he debated cutting the saddle cinches of the whole party, until with a grin he pulled out the saddles belonging to Vargas and Tyson.

Turning them over, he opened the larger blade of his battered old Barlow knife and sliced through the leather close to where it ran into the stitching of the skirt. Leaving a bare half-inch of leather connecting the cinch to the saddle, he returned them to the place where their owners had left them and swung lightly into the saddle of the pinto.

Moving easily, he herded the party's mounts in front of him, driving and scattering them downhill, towards the river sparkling in its pretty valley some miles away. Wheeler nodded with satisfaction as he saw the tired ponies line out down the slope.

'They ain't gonna stop 'til they reach water,' he informed himself, 'and unless them boys look sharp, they'll be ridin' Shanks's mare back to town.'

Turning back uphill, Wheeler carefully skirted the posse's camp, now in an uproar over the loss of their ponies and once out of earshot, he put the little mustang into an easy lope, the sort of pace a range-bred horse like this could keep up all day without turning a hair.

But Wheeler was too wise to tire his little mount unnecessarily and full dark saw the pony rubbed down, watered and snubbed to a big pine where he was chewing his way, slow but thorough, through a short measure of oats.

'Can't expect no one to work without decent feeding,' Wheeler informed the pony, as he prepared his own cold meal. The man from El Paso grimaced. 'Hard tack an' jerky sure goes down easier with coffee,' he explained to the pony, 'but I can't risk a fire.' The little animal snorted into his nosebag and Wheeler grinned.

'There ain't no more and you better get some sleep. We got some ridin' to do the next coupla days.' He paused looking up at the night sky and yards away in the brush, a squirrel started nervously before moving on about his nightly business.

Someone, somewhere in the darkness was whistling 'Shenendoah'.

CHAPTER TEN

Daylight found Cord Wheeler and the little pinto following a faint trail north through the high pine woods. His plan, such as it was, was simple. Whoever had killed Elford and framed Lou Underwood hadn't done it for fun. And Elford's rustling organization looked like the best place to look for his killer, which meant figuring out how they worked the cattle drive.

Jesse Wrawlings had claimed that he was losing cows, even though he couldn't find any cow trail leading off his spread. That was impossible. Any time a cow or horse or man moved they left some sign on the earth for a man to read. So there was a trail but perhaps, just perhaps, Wrawlings and his crew had seen the trail and not realized what they were looking at. Wrawlings and his men had been looking for a trail a thousand cows wide leading away from the ranches, probably heading down south. He hadn't been looking for a trail of twenty to fifty cows, with horses, driving between ranches. Specifically, between the other ranches and the B H B.

So Wheeler had figured and that was why he'd

headed north, riding in a big sweep which followed the borders between what had once been Jase Elford's rock and sand strewn wilderness and the more productive ranches to the south.

And along about noon of the second day, he'd found what he was looking for, on the sandy bottom of a little canyon, on Bar U land which bordered the B H B.

'Sure looks like mebbe we got lucky, li'l hoss,' Wheeler offered, as he gazed down at the welter of horse and cow tracks that defaced the sandy floor of the little canyon.

'And they're either real careless or . . . they ain't got no reason to worry about coverin' their tracks. Leastways,' he finished shrewdly, 'not here.'

Without haste, he backed his mount away from the tracks and secured him to a low growing piñon bush. Back at the mouth of the canyon, he crouched above the tracks, studying carefully.

'Two riders,' he decided, 'moving easy and heading onto B H B range. Hell, they could even have been drivin' in daylight and nobody would've turned a hair.'

Swinging into the saddle, he started the little pinto moving along the cow trail, reaching down as he did so to loosen his borrowed carbine in its saddle boot. After all, a man couldn't be too careful.

Wheeler, however, wasn't quite careful enough. He was following the trail, plainly enough marked, even where it passed over the occasional rock patch and, as it was getting late, he decided to turn off and make camp for the night. When he came to this decision, he was passing through another of the innumerable narrow canyons which the cow thieves seemed to favour for covering the route to their hideout, when he found himself turning a corner and topping a rise in the trail almost before he knew it, only to find the rustlers' hideout laid out before him.

Or, at least, if it wasn't a rustler's hideout, it should have been because it was perfectly suited for the job.

The man from El Paso found himself looking down in to a biggish valley, maybe twenty miles across the rim.

In the distance, at considerably less than a long rifle shot, a small lake sparkled in the late afternoon sunlight and by squinting hard, Wheeler could just make out the tiny feeder stream that flowed into it from the mountains. Lush grass, with here and there a bunch of lazy cows grazing, carpeted the floor as far as Wheeler could see and near the wide, flat beaten trail that led down from the rim was a substantial cabin and a pair of large, solidly made corrals, the nearest containing some twenty cows with their calves, while three saddle horses occupied the second.

From their size, the calves would be with their mothers for some months to come and Wheeler considered why a rustling outfit should go to the trouble of penning those few animals away from the rest, although even while this flashed across his mind he was swinging the pinto desperately in his tracks and urging him back down the trail, because there were two men sitting on the rails of the horse corral, plainly deep in talk.

Working rapidly, Wheeler hid the pinto away from the trail, before taking his borrowed carbine and moving, Indian quiet, back to the rim.

Neither man had moved from the corral rail and Wheeler watched until dark without catching a glimpse of the owner of the third horse. On his way back to collect his pony, when darkness had made further observation impossible, Wheeler gave a mental shrug. Beggars couldn't be choosers and somehow he had to get a look at those cows as well as searching the cabin for some sign of Elford's partner. Because partner he had to have.

The organization of the rustling operation was fairly clear to Wheeler, but there had to be someone in overall charge on this range, someone to have the cattle ready for Elford's trail crews and forged documents, someone to organize the collection of the cows and their rebranding, and all the other myriad details that would be beyond even the most expert cow man. No, Wheeler decided, this caused for expertise of a quite different sort.

'And it ain't either o' them two,' he decided, under his breath, as he looked carefully through the window of the cabin in the little valley, later that night.

They were just ordinary, forty and found cow hands, a white man and a Mexican with what looked like a dash of Indian in him, playing cards to pass the time and as luck would have it, from somewhere, they'd found a bottle. As Wheeler studied the pair through the window, the white man rose unsteadily and, giving the invariable male excuse, staggered towards the door.

He had barely fumbled his way into the enveloping darkness, when an expertly applied gun butt removed any interest he may have had in subsequent events.

Swiftly, Wheeler tied the man's hands and feet, having learnt the hard way not to leave an unsecured enemy behind him. Stepping past his victim, he paused just out of the light from the doorway and called blearily, 'Hey, ge' out here and loo' at this!'

With a muttered curse, the half-breed staggered to his feet and slouched across the floor, only to pause in the doorway.

Blearily, he stared into the darkness, then realization dawned and instinct sent his hand flashing to the long-bladed fighting knife he wore. But the knife was barely half out of its sheath, when Wheeler's rock-like fist crashed into his jaw, flinging him backwards into the cabin, stunned but still conscious.

Almost before his victim hit the floor, Wheeler sprang into the cabin and, as the man raised his head, the detective's fist smashed into his jaw again. The half-breed slumped, clearly out cold and Wheeler shook his head in disgust as his fingers busied themselves with trussing the man.

'I gotta find some other line of work,' he told himself disgustedly, ' 'cause I must be losin' my punch. I ain't never had to hit one o' them more'n once.'

His work on the half-breed finished, Wheeler moved the man's partner into the cabin and secured one man to the now cooling stove and the other to one of the bunks which had been fixed to the wall. As a final precaution, he gagged and blindfolded both men.

'I'm figgerin' that should hold 'em,' he muttered to himself, as he slipped silently into the moon shadow by the wall of the hut.

Thirty minutes later, assured that the owner of the third horse wasn't in the vicinity of the cabin, Wheeler approached the cows in the larger of the two corrals. Moonlight glimmered conveniently on the side of a cow and her baby who stood near the fence and Wheeler bit down a baffled curse at what he saw. Plain on the side of the cow was burned Jase Elford's B H B brand, while on what was clearly her calf was stamped Cal Underwood's Bar U.

For a moment, Wheeler's mind churned, turning over the implications of his study. Then, he grunted and swung himself up and onto the top rail. From this higher vantage point and with the benefit of a different angle, it was obvious to Wheeler's range-wise perception that the calf wasn't more than a month or two old and that the brand had been done less than three days before. It was careless work too, the edges of the scar had been burned too deep and looked red and sore, even in the moonlight, while its mother's brand was old and well healed.

'Now why in hell . . .' Wheeler began, shoving his battered Stetson to the back of his head in perplexity, but he was interrupted by the familiar sound of a Colt coming to full cock and a liquid voice saying, 'Mebbe you better ask Vargas when he gets here, *amigo*. Bu' for now, get down off the fence, *por favor*.'

Carefully, Wheeler twisted to face his captor, who

proved to be a slim Mexican, wearing a cheerful grin, belied by the wicked gleam of animal cruelty in the dark eyes. Looking beyond him, Wheeler saw a rifle propped against a tree next to a patient little burro with the flayed carcass of a deer across its withers, wordlessly explaining the previous absence of this, the third man. The Colt twitched minutely.

'I am not a patient man,' the Mexican said, moving slightly sideways. 'An' if you don' come down by yourself . . . I can always knock you down.'

'Don't you make no sudden moves, greaser,' Wheeler said nervously, 'I don't like loud noises.'

The Mexican nodded. 'I don' thin' that is gonna be a problem for you much longer, *señor*. Where are Jose and Carter?' he snapped.

Nervously, Wheeler raised his hands before whining, 'They got kinda tied up. I never hurt 'em, though. You ain't gonna do nothin' to me, are you, greaser?' The second use of the epithet brought a tightness to the man's lips, which Wheeler noted with grim satisfaction. An angry enemy is liable to be careless. But when the man spoke next, his tone was level, almost cold.

'You didn't hurt them, huh, *gringo*,' he began, smiling evilly. 'That may be a decision you come to regret, *amigo*.'

'You see this, you *gringo* pig?' the half-breed sneered, standing close enough to Wheeler to give him the benefit of a dose of old sweat and cheap whiskey and shaking a long lashed bull whip under his nose.

Wheeler's captor had made short work of rousing

his compatriots, after searching Wheeler and tying him to a rickety chair. Fortunately, the man's search had missed the little blade in the wrist sheath and Wheeler had just managed to palm it and was work-ing on the ropes when the half breed he'd dealt with earlier stumbled across the room.

'You know what I'm gonna do with this when Billy's finished with you?' the 'breed went on. 'First, I'm gonna take an eye out, then mebbe I take the other eye out.' The man leaned close and it took all of Wheeler's control to keep from retching in disgust as the man whispered, 'You know what it is like to feel the lash, to even know it is coming, but not to know where . . . ?'

'Pl . . . please, mister,' Wheeler began to babble frantically, looking beseechingly at the other white man, Carter. 'You wouldn't let them do that to one of your own kind, would you, mister, not another white man?'

'Ain't he a case?' Carter demanded of the room in general. 'It don't make no never mind to me what you are, mister,' he went on, addressing Wheeler, 'ol' Jose's gonna skin you out good.' He paused to throw another glass of liquor down his throat and slurred, 'Come an' ha' a drink, Jose, afore he wets his pants.'

As the Mexican turned away, the razor sharp little knife in Wheeler's hand sliced through the final strand of rope and Wheeler made a quick calcula-tion.

Gomez, his captor, had been gone well over an hour, maybe two, having left with the stated intention of locating the rest of the B H B posse members and finding out from Billy or his brother what was to be done with Wheeler. Probably not long enough to have found the posse, although not impossible. Balanced against the possibility of Gomez's return, was the longer the two men left behind kept drinking, the easier they would be to deal with. Wheeler shrugged. These two weren't that much of problem stone cold sober. He raised his voice and the words were cold and crisp and stung like a lash.

'Hey, you fat-lipped greaser bastard, give me a drink o' water and keep your filthy paws out of it!'

Mouthing curses, Jose erupted from his seat, to come and thrust his face within an inch of Wheeler's. Whatever the man was going to say was lost to posterity, because before he could speak, Wheeler's hands had flashed from behind him, grasping the half-breed by the ears, while his forehead smashed into the man's nose, bringing a satisfying crunch of bone.

With a massive shove, Wheeler sent the half-breed one way, jerking himself off the chair and throwing while he was in the air.

Half risen from his chair, the knife caught Carter in the chest and he collapsed across the table, his gun falling from his hand.

Wheeler wasted no time. He jerked his knife free as he vaulted the fallen table, scooping up his gunbelt as he jerked the door open.

'Don't look like it's your night, *amigo*,' Gomez's voice lisped from the darkness.

'Ain't that a fact,' the voice of Billy Vargas agreed, before adding, 'Bad luck, Mr Wheeler.'

CHAPTER ELEVEN

For a bare split second, Wheeler calculated the odds, poised to see if his speed of hand and skill with a pistol would stand the test. Then, he caught sight of a white-faced Delia Underwood, listless and drooping in the saddle, her brother Lou sitting his pony next to her. Vargas followed the direction of Wheeler's gaze.

'You're right,' he grinned. 'You pull on us and the first one gets it is her. 'Course,' he leered, 'she may thank you in the long run on account o' what me and the boys got planned for a little later.'

Framed in the doorway, Wheeler seemed to slump.

'Guess you got me, l'il Billy,' he managed to grin, then seeing the anger in the young man's face, added kindly, 'Don't worry, size ain't everything.'

Flushing hotly, Vargas bellowed, 'Lock the three of 'em in the storehouse 'round back.'

Grinning despite himself, Gomez slid from his horse and said silkily, 'The *pistola, señor.*'

Indolently, Wheeler flipped the holstered weapon in the man's direction and, as Gomez bent to catch it, the detective swept both hands behind his back and smoothly sheathed his little blade.

'We hadn't seen anyone for days, so I suppose we got careless,' Delia Underwood explained ruefully. 'We were just riding down this little canyon on the B Bar B, I think, and they . . . well . . . they just appeared,' she finished helplessly.

'Well, I guess it can't be helped,' Wheeler shrugged, settling back in the darkness. 'Now, afore this scum bed down for the night, they're probably gonna come and check on us. Now, when they do, Miz Delia, this is what you do,' he began, bringing his hands in front of him and eyeing the contents of the store shed's shelves.

It was Billy Vargas himself, accompanied by Gomez and the half-breed, who came at last, peering into the darkness with a vicious leer. Cursorily, he checked the ropes on both men before demanding, 'Now where at's that little lady?'

Wheeler, who had nearly broken a wrist retying his severed bonds, jerked up his head and snapped, 'Why?'

Vargas eyed his prisoner contemptuously.

'Now, why'd you think, Fancy Pants?' he began.

'Truth is, *gringo*,' Gomez interrupted, pulling out a peculiarly shaped tobacco pouch, made from some sort of tanned skin, and carefully rolling a brown-paper cigarette, 'we got a little . . . uh . . . how you say . . . party planned and the *señorita* is gonna be the main entertainment.'

Wheeler nodded. 'Somethin' like that Apache woman?' he asked mildly, indicating the tobacco pouch, 'or was it Comanche?'

Gomez shrugged. 'Kiowa,' he admitted, and Wheeler shook his head in mock admiration.

'Kiowa,' he repeated. 'I wouldn't've figgered you had the nerve. Or was she dead when you found her?'

For a long second Gomez studied the detective, then his breath erupted in a long sigh and, as the sweat beads broke out on his forehead, he whispered, 'Keep it up, *gringo*. Talk all you want. Soon you only gonna have breath for screaming.'

Abruptly impatient, Vargas snapped, 'Enough o' that. Where's the girl?'

Wheeler jerked his head backwards. 'I wouldn't get too close was I you,' the detective offered. 'She's real sick.'

With a doubtful look in Wheeler's direction, Vargas, stepped forward, raising the lantern he was carrying as he did so. Lamplight splashed across the white face and straining eyes of a delirious Delia Underwood. Seeing the light, she strained towards it, squirming deeper into the foul-smelling black vomit that covered her bed, and dribbling black filth from her mouth.

'Help me,' she gasped, but the voice was a mere parody of a human beings.

Without a second look, Vargas snatched backwards, blurting as he did so, 'Christ, it's cholera!'

'*Madre de Dios*,' Gomez blurted, swiftly crossing himself as the pair backed out of the little hut.

'Hey,' Wheeler bellowed, choking hard to keep back the laughter. 'You can't leave us here with her. We'll get it!' he finished, voice rising to a scream.

But the evening's surprises didn't all go one way. As if in answer to Wheeler's call, the door slammed open and Gomez's voice said, 'Don't worry about the cholera, *señors*, I brought someone to keep you company. Get in here . . . Señor Boss!' the Mexican sneered.

There was the sound of a heavy body falling, a door slammed shut and the group were left alone in the fetid darkness.

For a long moment there was silence, then Cal Underwood's voice said shakily, 'Can someone tell me how my daughter is?'

'Not sure how that goddamn Cord Wheeler manages to smoke these disgusting things,' came the surprising answer.

'It's 'cause I smoke 'em, not chew 'em, Miz Delia,' Wheeler answered with a chuckle.

'Phew, I don't reckon you ever gonna get that smell out of your clothes, Sis,' Lou Underwood offered as he carefully examined the area outside the dirty glass of the storeroom window.

'Ain't but one I can see,' he went on before the girl could reply.

'It had to smell bad,' Wheeler explained, slicing through the last of the ropes that pinioned Cal Underwood's legs, ' 'cause that's how cholera takes a person and horse sh— sign was the only thing I could get. Couldn't take a chance nearer the house. Where is he, Lou?' the detective went on. 'Can you see who it is?'

'Nope,' the boy admitted, 'but he's on the small side.'

'OK, just keep watchin' him,' Wheeler answered, busy with the door.

'Before you go, Mr Wheeler,' Delia Underwood asked, 'what was that business with that foul Mexican, about the Kiowa woman? I heard it but I didn't understand it.'

'Don't often see 'em these days,' Wheeler answered abstractedly, busy with his silent work on the door. 'He had a tobacco pouch made from the Kiowa woman's breast.' For a moment, Wheeler turned and the red, killing light flared behind his eyes.

'So you just remember that if you ever get your rifle sights square on his chest. Now,' he ordered, 'don't make no more noise.'

There was a soft click and Wheeler carefully eased the door open a few inches, dropping to the floor as he did so. Seconds later he was up and, signalling for the others to remain where they were, he slipped out in to the moonless night.

Breathing a small sigh of relief that the surface was grass and not light desert sand which would have outlined him clearly to his enemy, Wheeler eased forward silently until he was within a few feet of the beat the sentry had selected for himself.

Watching from the window, Lou Underwood saw the sentry pass. As the man did so, a black shape rose from the ground, joining with the sentry. There was a minute flash of light and then the double shape collapsed, only for a shadow to detach itself from the bundle and run, swiftly and silently to the corner of the house and out of Lou's sight.

After what seemed like an eternity, Wheeler eased back through the door and whispered, 'One sentry. Lucky for me, he had this,' he continued, buckling on his weapon belt, before adding, 'Looks like the rest of 'em are drunk.' A moment later the moon crested a low hill.

'Good.' Wheeler nodded his satisfaction. 'We're gonna need some light to work by. Get the ponies.'

Jose couldn't sleep. Hardly surprising, when one considers the crude and clumsy attempts by his friends to treat his broken and badly mangled nose. No position seemed comfortable and giving it up as a bad job, he rose, deciding to take a *pasear* in the moonlight.

Collecting his whip but not bothering with the gunbelt, Jose jerked open the door, only to be confronted by the man who had given him his nose, quietly leading Billy Vargas's favourite mount out of the horse corral. And his back was to the cabin. And to the half-breed.

The first thing Wheeler knew about Jose's insomnia was when the half-breed's whip sliced into his back. Pain nearly made Wheeler black out, but he jerked around, reaching for his pistol, and almost immediately abandoned the idea.

The whip flicked towards him again and Wheeler leaped backwards, releasing the pony as he did so and moving round the crude corral, so as to lead Jose past the gate. Leering expectantly, the Mexican moved forward, flicking the whip behind him, so as to aim his stroke.

'I'm gonna enjoy this, *gringo*,' he began, 'and you better be quiet, 'less you want the others spoiling the party!' At the last word, his hand jerked, but instead of the whip shooting forward to slash and rip, nothing happened. The whip was stuck, caught somewhere behind him.

Twisting rapidly, Jose jerked at the rawhide, then stopped, staring in disbelief at the sight of the *gringo señorita* who had been dying of cholera, now fully recovered and standing with one dainty foot across the braided rawhide of his beloved whip.

With a scream of bestial rage, the half-breed dropped the handle and sprang towards the woman. Which was where he made the final mistake of a largely misspent life. He forgot Cord Wheeler.

Jose was a bare two feet from the cringing, terrified girl, when he felt a strong leather band circle his neck and jerk tight. Tearing and struggling, fighting for breath, he clawed at the vicious band as the lights flashed green and red before his terrified glare.

Two minutes later, Wheeler took his knee out of the back of Jose's stiffening corpse and dropped it and the whip into the dust of the corral.

'I feel sick,' Delia Underwood began.

'No time for that,' Wheeler snapped, as he bent and began to drag the body downwind of the increasingly edgy remuda. 'Help Lou and your pa with the ponies.'

'But—' she began.

'No time for that, either,' Wheeler interrupted swiftly.' Get the ponies, but before you do, get my carbine. Them boys sound like they're waking up!'

Delia Underwood was halfway to the horse gear stacked against a convenient post, when the door of the cabin burst open and one of the rustlers stood framed in the moonlight-flooded doorway.

In a single flashing glance he took in the scene in the corral and his hand was driving for his gun, when the first bullet from Wheeler's pistol smashed into his chest, throwing him back into the cabin.

Wheeler didn't wait to see who else might appear, he simply emptied the Smith & Wesson through the rapidly closing door then opened his mouth to bellow for his carbine, only to shut it again as he caught sight of Delia, the reins of her borrowed mount wrapped round one arm and the lever of her little Winchester blurring as she pumped lead through the door and window of the cabin.

Momentarily, she paused and Lou Underwood's voice rang through the echoing stillness. 'Yeehah,' he bellowed, driving what was left of the riderless remuda up the slope before him as Wheeler ran towards his saddled but restless pony.

Without taking her eyes from the cabin door, the girl snatched the reins and swung aboard her frightened mount, pulling him sharply round and sweeping after her father and brother, as Wheeler, with a hand on the pommel and one foot in the stirrup, kneed his pony into a fast lope, following the girl up the trail.

Suddenly, she screamed. Wheeler's foot had slipped from the stirrup and his suddenly shifting weight was dragging the pony almost to a standstill, as the B H B men poured from the cabin and guns began to speak in the night-time stillness.

CHAPTER TWELVE

Of course, that should have been it. Everyone's luck runs out, Wheeler admitted to himself, bracing for the impact of lead, as he fought with his terrified pony and the B H B bullets pecked nearer.

But just as a slug whined from a rock, barely a yard from the detective's boot, there came an answering hail of lead and Wheeler looked up to see the three Underwoods, off their ponies and blazing away at the rustlers.

And they weren't wasting many cartridges. Wheeler saw one man blasted backwards and Billy Vargas diving frantically for cover as another bullet snatched off his greasy Stetson. Then Wheeler was in the saddle, dragging his pony round by brute force and kicking him into a gallop up the trail.

Slapping with reins and kicking, Wheeler urged the game little mustang onwards as Cal Underwood and the twins mounted and headed up the trail in front of him.

Suddenly, as Wheeler topped the rim and began the rocky descent through the narrow canyon where he'd entered the valley, he felt his mount lurch as simultaneously, there came the whomp of a striking bullet. For some seconds, the gallant little mustang raced on, then suddenly, there was blood flying from his nose and mouth and even as the detective eased back on the reins, he staggered and almost fell.

Wheeler was out of the saddle in an instant but one glance told him it was no use. The pony gazed at him from pain-racked eyes as the blood flowed sluggishly from mouth and nostrils and Wheeler reached up to gently rub at the flattened ears as his other hand sought for the butt of his Smith & Wesson.

'What happened?' Lou Underwood demanded, as he drew rein next to Wheeler, leapt down and began to help drag the riding gear off the dead pony.

'Shot in the lungs,' Wheeler answered, freeing the last strap and reaching for a pistol as Underwood and his daughter loped up.

'We missed you in the dark,' Underwood explained.

'You should ha' kept goin',' Wheeler stated ungraciously. 'I ain't anxious for that crowd to get anywhere near Miz Delia.'

'Miz Delia can take care of herself!' the girl snapped, nervous fingers tapping at her saddle-booted Winchester.

'Ain't no doubt o' that,' Wheeler admitted, 'but we're short of cartridges, and ain't got no grub.'

'Lou,' he went on, 'skin out the haunch o' that pony and cut off enough meat to last the four of us about three, four days. Don't bother with no more 'cause it won't keep. ' He stooped, making a minute adjustment to the Apache moccasins that he wore, then rose and loped easily away up the slope. The girl looked after him, wondering. Someone, somewhere was whistling 'Shenendoah.'

The scene around the cabin was one of utter chaos. Lou had made a good job of getting the pony herd out of the corral and up the trail because there wasn't a horse in sight. That should have left the gang on foot and unable to follow but, as the detective watched, a beautiful palamino trotted up to the smaller of the two corrals. Even at that distance, Wheeler recognized the slim shape of the Mexican Gomez and he nodded to himself.

'Allus figure that one to have an ace up his sleeve,' Wheeler muttered, impressed despite himself.

Abruptly, the palamino was jerked away from the corral and headed out into the valley, plainly heading for a source of horse flesh that Wheeler had known nothing about.

In a single movement, Wheeler was on his feet and heading back to his companions.

'I figure we got an hour, now, mebbe less,' Wheeler finished, easing tight the last strap on Cal Underwood's saddle and swinging up behind the rancher.

'You and Miz Delia head for the ranch,' Wheeler went on. 'With Vargas and his boys gone, you can fort up there 'til your dad arrives and then you can head for town.'

'And what about you?' the girl demanded.

'Me?' Wheeler asked innocently. 'Oh, I'm going skunk killin'.'

Some hours later, just as the sun said noon, Gomez pulled his palamino roughly to a halt and stared down at the welter of tracks which appeared to lead into the mouth of one of the innumerable little canyons that made up most of the landscape.

'What you waitin' for?' demanded Billy Vargas, as he pulled up next to him.

'I don' know,' Gomez shrugged. 'This don' look right. We been followin' these *hombres* an' the *señorita* long time an' they ain't never showed more'n a hoof print. Rode on rock, swept their trail, all the things a man, a good man who knows the country would do. And now this. A plain trail, leading . . . mebbe leading where they want us to go.'

'I figger the greaser's had too much sun,' snapped Chet Harris, drawing rein on the other side of Vargas. 'Them tracks is fresh,' he went on, 'they ain't more'n mebbe half-hour ahead o' us. I say we push on.'

'No,' Gomez snapped. 'They use the old blanket trick to throw us off.' Both his companions looked blank and Gomez said impatiently, 'You lead the pony to a place where you want the *hombre* following to think you go. Then, you lead pony on to blanket so he don' leave no sign and head off some other way.' He saw the disbelief start on their faces and insisted, 'You give me a l'il while and I show you.'

'No,' said Rollins. 'We got a plain trail and I say we

foller it.' Abruptly, he jerked his mount round to face Gomez.

'And I don't aim to leave no thieving cowardly greaser behind us with a rifle.' Rollins's hand rose to hover over his gun butt. 'So you're comin' along!' he finished tautly.

For a moment, Gomez glared back at the hated *gringo*, then a smile stretched his mouth and he spread his hands.

'Sure,' he began. 'We all friends here . . .' But what he was going to say was lost in the crash of a shot, as his left hand, hidden by the turning of his mount, snatched a pistol from his belt and fired. Hit in the belly, Rollins slumped, falling from his mount as his killer looked on, eyes gleaming with pleasure and hatred.

'Don' worry, *amigo*,' Gomez laughed, as the rest of the gang rode up, swinging into a circle behind Vargas. 'He will take only a day, maybe two, to die and then you can look for the *gringo* again. Me, I thin' I look . . . this way,' he finished, swinging his pony and sending it up the rock and piñon-clad slope.

Looking down, Rat Ferris, late of Jesse Wrawlings' O Bar O, grimaced, and said, 'What d'we do about Chet?'

'He ain't gotta chance,' Vargas stated bluntly, 'and we gotta get after that goddam detective,' he said, indicating the plain trail into the canyon. 'Leave him his Colt and a canteen, 'less you feel like finishin' him yourself.'

Ferris looked up with a sneer. 'What, wi' cartridges

the price they are?' he demanded callously.

'Never figgered to fool the greaser,' Wheeler stated, as he and Underwood watched the palamino breast the top of the rise and begin to circle, as its rider searched for tracks. 'But it don't look like any o' the rest of 'em think much of his tracking. Best we get moving, one pony ain't givin' us much of a start and it may take us a while to find what we want.'

'Don't seem like any sort of a start,' Underwood offered reasonably. 'What exactly are we looking for?'

'A good place to camp,' came the unexpected reply.

'Looks like the greaser was right,' Ferris said, spitting disgustedly. 'What d'we do now?'

Vargas didn't answer, staring perplexedly at the rock fall, extending fifty feet up the walls of the canyon, which the gang had entered a bare half-hour before. Plainly, neither man nor horse could have passed this way and the rustler boss, never the clearest of thinkers, found himself momentarily at a loss. But it was only for a moment.

Turning to Ferris, Vargas snapped, 'Take Vittorio, Phillipe and Mocha, get back down the trail and follow that greaser Gomez. If he finds them three and the girl, kill the men and bring the girl back. Oh, and Rat,' he finished, as Ferris turned away, 'if there's one thing I can't stand, it's a smart greaser. So you can shoot that yellar bastard, too.'

'Pleasure,' Ferris sneered. 'Never could stand the

bastard myself.' Another thought struck and he demanded suspiciously, 'Where you an' the others gonna be?'

'Oh, we got another l'il bet to cover,' replied his esteemed boss.

Sunset was just gilding the tops of the nearby peaks as Gomez crested a last ridge, only to snatch desperately at the reins as he all but threw himself from the saddle.

Swiftly caching the palomino, he ran back up the trail, throwing himself down to crawl the last few yards as he reached the top. What he saw there brought a wicked grin of satisfaction. The party he was following had apparently found a comfortable spot for the night, in the clear space before an opening in the hillside that looked like an old mine working.

Already two of them were stretched in their blankets, while the others, Wheeler and the older man Gomez guessed, were sitting, also blanket wrapped, on a convenient log facing the mine entrance, unable to see their would-be killer as he peered across the 400 yards that separated him from his victims.

'Easy as taking a drink,' Gomez muttered to himself, pulling up his battered Spencer and carefully setting the sights.

Strangely, the *gringos* couldn't have been expecting an attack, because, although his first shot tumbled the figure wearing Cord Wheeler's battered Stetson into the fire, the second figure hadn't moved when the Spencer's second massive .52 calibre slug tore into it. But Gomez had no time for thinking. One of those blanket-wrapped shapes had to be the girl and there was no way he wanted to put a bullet into such a tasty little morsel, even to keep her from running away, although, he conjectured lewdly as he ran, breathless and sweating towards the camp ground, a bullet in the leg wouldn't spoil her usefulness for other things.

But as he topped the slight rise that led into the campsite, his instinct, honed by years of devilry, belatedly began screaming a warning at him. The Stetson topped first figure was still lying across the fire and gently smouldering. Smouldering because that's what mesquite does if you wrap it in a blanket and then knock it into a fire.

For an instant, Gomez stared at the blanket wrapped dummy, unable to believe he had fallen for such a simple trick. Then a noise behind him, a soft whistling, spun him round and he found himself face to face with the lean *gringo* with the cold green eyes.

'Fill your hand, greaser,' Wheeler ordered softly. 'You've just naturally played out your string.'

'But, *amigo*,' Gomez began, half turning away and dropping his left hand out of sight. Two shots cracked into the twilight stillness, sounding so close together as to appear one, then Wheeler walked towards his victim, wiping at the blood which dribbled sluggishly from the fresh wound on his cheek. Callously, he shoved a foot under the Mexican's ribs and flipped him over. Any check would have been superfluous, the heavy slug from the Smith & Wesson had torn a fist-sized hole in Gomez's chest.

'Tricky yeller bastard,' Wheeler said softly, spitting on the up-turned face, 'but, this time, not tricky enough.'

Struck by a chord of memory, Wheeler squatted, searching the man's pockets only to be interrupted by Underwood appearing out of the gloom.

'Look around, will you, Cal?' Wheeler asked, still busy with his search. 'The greaser's got a horse cached somewhere and we can sure use him.' The rancher nodded shortly, turning to go, only to draw up short at Wheeler's grunt of satisfaction.

Looking back, Underwood saw Wheeler rise to his feet, clutching the tobacco pouch that had belonged to the vicious Mexican. Unaware that he was being watched, Wheeler walked to the scrubby cottonwood that clung to life at the entrance of the mine and, almost reverently, emptied out the tobacco and then carefully hung the pouch in the tree, where sun and wind and the meagre South-Western rain would return it to the earth. For a moment, he was still, intoning a few words in the guttural Apache of the border, before turning away.

Underwood, unseen outside the reach of the fire-light, shook his head in wonderment that almost amounted to disbelief.

'You sure never can tell about a feller . . .' he began, as he breasted the rise where the late and unlamented Gomez had first observed the camp-fire scene that had been staged entirely for his benefit. But what he saw from there, a bare mile away down

the trail, threw all thoughts of Wheeler and his idio-
syncrasies aside.

Desperately, he tore back down the slope, sped by
a bullet that pecked at his heels. Wheeler had to
know about this and fast.

CHAPTER THIRTEEN

'They . . . they's . . . someone camped on our trail,' Underwood blurted. 'An' . . . An' . . . they took a shot at me!'

'Stay here!' Wheeler snapped, scooping up his borrowed carbine and heading for the slope at a fast run.

It wasn't quite as bad as Underwood's excited warning had made it seem. But, Wheeler admitted ruefully to himself, it was bad enough.

In the distance, at well over a long rifle shot, the man from El Paso could see the glimmering ember that represented the rustlers' fire, outlining the figure of the sentry who stood between, now and then scanning the skyline in Wheeler's direction. The position of the camp had been shrewdly chosen, close enough to the trail to detect anyone leaving in that direction, as long as the sentry was awake, but far enough away and well enough hidden for a surprise attack by any party following the rustlers to be well nigh impossible.

Wheeler grunted disdainfully. Normally, a sentry a man could see was worse than useless but in this case he had obviously been placed so that he couldn't be surprised. All they had to do now, Wheeler admitted to himself, was wait until dawn, then ride in and sweep Underwood and Wheeler, short of cartridges as they were, into their net. Unless . . . Abruptly, Wheeler jerked backwards. If there was any coal oil in the old lamp he had spotted at the entrance to the workings, he and the old man might still win out yet.

Rat Ferris wasn't an individual given to early rising, but this morning, he was awake and in the saddle before the sun had begun to top the horizon.

'You figger mebbe they ain't gonna be expectin' us, *amigo*?' Phillipe demanded as he drew rein next to the despised *gringo*.

'If Mocha had had more sense, and used a knife instead o' throwing lead last night,' Ferris grumbled, 'we'd have one less to worry about now. Well,' he went on, as the squat Mexican slipped silently over the rise that hid Wheeler and Underwood's camp from view, 'What'd you find out, you little bastard?'

Apparently ignoring Ferris's insult, the squat little Mexican leered villainously and said, 'I find out that their sentry, he is asleep but now . . .' – the little killer indicated the empty sheath at his side – 'he ain't gonna wake up no more.'

His companions grinned and even Ferris unbent enough to say, 'Good work, Mocha.' The white man paused, thinking, then said, 'No reason I can see why we shouldn't just sneak down there, quiet like, walk the horses right up to 'em and blast 'em to kingdom come.'

'Sounds good to me, *amigo*,' Phillipe sneered,

drawing his Colt and beginning to check the loads.

Nothing appeared to have changed from the description Mocha had given the gang as their horses topped the rise in the trail and began the gentle descent towards the camp ground. No jingle of harness or rattle of weapons betrayed them until Ferris, who was in the lead, got to within fifty yards of the low burning fire and found his mount pushing noisily through a collection of dried mesquite. Cursing softly, he eased the pony through the obstacle, gesturing the others to silence, and in his preoccupation, not noticing that this line of tinder-dry branches surrounded the whole camp. And, of course, in the pre-dawn chill, he missed the stink of coal oil.

Gesturing his men to silence, he carefully eased his pistol from its holster, took aim and fired into the nearest blanket-wrapped shape, the one with Cord Wheeler's Stetson balanced across where the nose should have been.

Without waiting for any further orders, his men followed suit, Mocha even jumping down and running across to retrieve his knife from the sentry.

With a wicked leer, the squat *bandido* flipped back the blanket from the still form, only to snatch back his hand in horror. The face he found himself looking down into was that of Gomez. And, before he could collect his thoughts or begin to work out why his erstwhile comrade, who had clearly been dead a long time before Mocha's knife had pierced his lung, should be lying here, a voice split the rapidly lightening dawn air.

115

'Put down your guns, boys. I don't want to have to kill you.'

In answer, Ferris instantly threw up his Colt and fired blindly in the direction he thought the voice had come from. Level with his fourth shot, there was the crack of a Winchester and Ferris crumpled, shot through the chest, dying as he fell. But the shot had served its purpose, locating the hidden rifleman in the mouth of the cave.

Almost as one man the remaining *bandidos* opened fire, falling back towards the only natural cover, the thin line of mesquite branches. As Mocha, the first man to reach it, flopped down behind the flimsy covering, he abruptly raised up in disgust. Something, something oily and disgusting, covered the branches and, as he opened his mouth to yell, Cord Wheeler, using the last bullet in the magazine of Gomez's Spencer, fired into the little pouch of gunpowder hanging from the bush next to the squat bandido's head.

Instantly, the gunpowder spouted into flame and the coal oil-soaked sticks erupted, engulfing Mocha's face and chest in their midst. The squat little man screamed and Cal Underwood, driven almost mad by a heady mixture of fear and excitement, leapt to his feet, firing his last cartridge in the little man's direction.

Underwood's shot missed but Phillipe wasn't so careless, jerking up his Colt as he ran forward and driving a bullet into the old man's shoulder, sending him spinning away in to the darkness of the cave, where he and Wheeler had sheltered.

It was Phillipe's last act on earth, because as he thumb-cocked the heavy Colt there was a flicker in the air and Wheeler's little blade buried itself to the hilt in the *bandido*'s throat. Which by Wheeler's count still left one.

Desperately, Wheeler dropped the empty Spencer and hurtled across the barrier which he and Underwood had erected in haste the night before, as Vittorio swung up his Colt. The Mexican's first shot smashed into a rock inches from Wheeler's foot, then Wheeler had Phillipe's Colt in his right hand, the heel of his left snapping back the hammer, driving three fast shots into Vittorio's chest and throwing the man backwards to lie still, dead before he hit the ground.

Slowly, like a man tired to death, Wheeler struggled to his feet, automatically checking the loads in his borrowed weapon before jerking the few remaining cartridges from Phillipe's belt to fill the empty chambers. Almost incidentally, he raised the gun and drove a merciful bullet in to the screaming, charred thing that had once been Mocha, the *bandido*, before turning to the cave mouth, where a low moaning told him that there was one at least alive enough to need his attention.

Noon heat was chasing away the shadows from their camping ground as Wheeler propped the palamino's saddle against a convenient rock and turned to inspect his patient, only to find Underwood awake and looking back at him.

Absently, Wheeler eased the unfamiliar Colt in his belt and moved silently across to where Underwood lay stretched under a blanket.

'How you feelin'?' the detective asked gently.

'Pretty good,' Underwood lied, stretching to raise himself, only to fall back with a grimace of pain.

'Yeah,' Wheeler offered sardonically. 'I can see how good you feel.' He paused, shifting his feet.

'See, the thing is, Cal,' he continued, indicating the bodies he had dragged some distance away from the fire, 'I made a count of our friends here and I figger that there's about five, mebbe six that ain't here and should be.'

'So we can expect more company any time,' Underwood groaned. 'You better prop me up in the mouth o' that cave, Cord. Then give me a rifle and get out. No point both of us gettin'—'

'I don't think it's quite that simple,' Wheeler interrupted mildly. 'We had enough trouble dealin' with four of them. If they were comin', why not come together? There'd be no point in waitin'.'

'No,' he went on thoughtfully, 'L'il Billy ain't here and that means he had another bet to cover. How far are we from your ranch, Cal?'

'Coupla days, the way them bastards'd go,' Underwood answered uneasily. 'A day, a long day, the way I'd go. Better travellin', too, good water for a noonin'. Are you figgerin' what I think you're figgerin', that them bastards have side tracked and headed for the ranch?'

'It'd be logical.' Wheeler shrugged. 'If Ferris and his boys had finished us, it's a good place to meet up. Plenty o' grub and cartridges if they want to hightail it. And on the off chance that Ferris and his *compañeros* didn't finish us, it's where we'd be most likely to go, bein' short on grub and cartridges, which he'd figger since we had to leave all our stuff back at their hideout.'

'Christ, Cord, what'll they do if they catch the kids. . . ?'

'Best you rest up,' Wheeler put in, ' 'cause come nightfall, we're headin' south to find out.'

Next day, dawn found Delia Underwood out of bed and shaking her brother awake.

'Get up, sleepy head,' she insisted tolerantly. 'If you want flapjacks for breakfast, I'm needin' a bucket of water. And you'd better see to those ponies.'

Twilight had all but given way to full dark as the pair of youngsters had ridden up to the door of the ranch house the previous night, only to find the place completely deserted.

'Must be all out huntin' me for the reward,' Lou offered cynically, after he'd checked the barn and bunkhouse.

But things always looked brighter in the morning and with the coming of daylight, Delia at least, was inclined to take a more optimistic view.

'Dad and Mr Wheeler'll be here today or mebbe tomorrow,' she assured her brother. 'Then we can get this whole mess straightened out. But for now, you're going to need another bucket of water.'

'Why?' Lou demanded carelessly.

'Because, Brother dear, dishes don't do themselves! Come on, hop to it.'

'Christ, I pity the fella you marry, you'll keep him

running round like a rat on a hot skillet,' the boy grumbled, as he grabbed up the bucket and made for the door.

Moments later, she heard his voice again.

'D, D, come out. . . .' Suddenly the words were cut off, then there was a gasp, cut off in mid cry and Lou was screaming, 'D, D run for it! They're he—' only for the words to be choked off in mid-sentence.

Without thinking, the girl snatched up her little saddle gun from its place by the door and wrenched the door open.

Hope died as she took in the scene. Lou lay sense-less or worse in the dust of the yard with a vicious-faced white man whom she recognized from the posse standing over him. Beyond him, three Mexicans sat their horses, smiling with callous satis-faction.

Desperately, she jerked up the rifle, lining it on the man standing over her brother.

'Get away from him!' she screamed, only to suddenly find the barrel of her weapon jerked upwards so viciously that the rifle was snatched out of her hands. She whirled, drawing back a fist to find herself confronted by Billy Vargas.

'Waal,' the young man sneered complacently, 'looks like we're gonna have our l'il party after all! ' His peace of mind didn't last long though because, without warning, Delia Underwood drove her fist, backed by all the weight of her muscular right arm, full into his nose, smashing it across his face like an overripe tomato.

CHAPTER FOURTEEN

'Now just so you and your punk brother understand, I'm gonna spell it out for you. Whatever happens we're gonna have a l'il party later. And you, darlin',' Billy Vargas sneered nasally, glaring down at the girl seated in an old battered armchair in the comfortable living-room of the ranch house, 'are gonna be the main attraction. I'd let the boys at you now, especially 'cause o' this,' he went on, indicating his much damaged nose, 'but you got a little job to do first.'

'I sent Rat and some o' the others to take care of your pa and that goddamn detective. But that Wheeler, he's tricky and he may give Rat the slip. In which case, I figger he'll come here. An' when he does, you're gonna sucker 'im for us.' The girl opened her mouth to speak, but Vargas forestalled her.

'An' if you was gonna say you won't do it, let me explain this to you. If I gotta get Wheeler and your pa myself, your brother's gonna be a long time dying . . . while you watch every minute. Do like I tell you and he'll get a bullet, clean.'

Vargas paused. 'Well, what d'you say?' he demanded.

For a moment, Delia thought madly of throwing the words back in his face. Only for a moment though, because suddenly she was back in that grubby little storeroom, with Cord Wheeler smearing her blankets with horse apples. She'd been frightened then, and to hide it, she'd demanded, 'Do you really think we've got a chance?'

Wheeler had smiled at her and said, 'As an old friend o' mine used to say, best we can do here is stay alive and wait for the cards to start running our way.' Seeing the look on her face, he sobered and went on gently, 'There's always a chance. The trick is to be ready when it comes along.'

Stay alive. And be ready. Slowly, she nodded then turned to look into Vargas' grinning face. Abruptly, she slumped, as though admitting defeat and whispered, 'Very well, since it looks like I have no option. But,' she went on as Vargas turned away triumphantly, 'I have your word that Lou'll be killed clean before . . . before you do whatever you have in mind for me?'

'Sure,' Vargas said easily, over his shoulder. 'You got my word he'll get a bullet,' pausing to add under his breath, 'eventually.'

For the group in the Underwood ranch house, the day dragged on interminably and it wasn't until the afternoon shadows were lengthening towards twilight, that one of the Mexicans, Enrique, watching the trail down from the bluff, hissed softly. Vargas was at his side in a moment and the grinning Mexican pointed towards the dusty trail that led down to the Underwood's horse corral and the thick planked horse trough between it and the house.

A figure, hatless and dishevelled, was staggering towards the trough and, as he drew closer, Vargas gave a vicious grunt of satisfaction.

'Waal, I'll be a sonovabitch,' he sneered, as the stumbling figure fell to its knees, 'if it ain't Mr Fancy Pants.'

Grinning his satisfaction, Vargas pushed through the door and almost ran to where Cord Wheeler, clearly using the last of his strength, was trying to lever himself up the side of the horse trough.

'W . . . w . . . water,' the man from El Paso gasped, lifting a hand to splash desperately in the trough containing the life-giving fluid.

Almost casually, Vargas reached out a hand and slammed his all but helpless victim back into the dust. Wheeler lay without moving, eyes closed. Motioning his men back, Vargas reached down and jerked his victim upright.

Turning to place himself between Wheeler and his men, Vargas slowly drew back one hand, closing it into a meaty fist as he said, 'I'm sure gonna enjoy this!'

But just as the big youngster's fist reached back to the full extent of his arm, Wheeler's eyes flashed open and his head jerked forward, catching Vargas a vicious butt precisely across the bridge of his already severely damaged nasal organ.

There was a flurry of swift movement and then the half-dazed Vargas found himself caught, pulled off

123

balance by a steely arm that all but closed his wind-
pipe while one of his own Colts was boring a hole
under his chin and an icy voice was saying softly,
'Easy all. Get rid of the hardware, boys, and your boss
might live to see the sunset.'

But the rustlers made no movement until Enrique
said, 'Wha' you wan' we should do, Billy?'

'Better tell 'em, l'il Billy,' Wheeler snapped. 'I'm
sure runnin' low on patience.'

'Look, fellas,' Vargas whined, 'you can see
how . . .' But he got no further, because at that
instant, he dropped all his weight on to the arm
Wheeler had round his neck, forcing the detective to
release his hold.

Vargas lurched forward, staggering clumsily as he
desperately tried to turn, only to be flung backwards
into the dust as Wheeler's first shot caught him high
in the shoulder, an awe-struck witness to the aston-
ishing scene that followed, as Wheeler dived towards
the horse trough, his left hand blurring the hammer
of his borrowed Colt.

Enrique's gun had barely cleared leather when
Wheeler's second shot smashed into the Mexican's
chest, throwing him into the dirt, as the detective's
third, a bare split second later, caught Williams, the
only white man, cleanly between the eyes, sending
the big rustler spinning backwards, his weapon,
barely clear of the holster, discharging harmlessly
into the ground.

The deaths of their *compañeros* was enough for the
remaining Mexicans. One turned and ran towards
the house while the second, showing more sense,

ducked towards the barn, clearly heading for the horses and swift escape.

Wheeler acted with characteristic ruthlessness.

Ignoring the moaning Vargas, he shifted round, propping both elbows on the worn rim of the trough and sending a shot in the direction of the man fleeing for the house. His bullet kicked dust short and a foot to the left of the runner and, cursing the short-barrelled Civilian model Colt, Wheeler shifted his aim minutely and squeezed off his last shot, this time catching the rustler square in the back and driving him forward to land, fatally wounded, in the dust of the threshold.

The sound of the shot had barely died away when an agonized groan snapped Wheeler round to where Billy Vargas, blood pumping from his badly wounded shoulder, was desperately scrabbling for his second pistol. In a single blur of movement, Wheeler flipped his empty Colt, caught the barrel and hurled the weapon straight at Vargas.

Caught full in the face by the two and half pound weight of the viciously flung Colt, Vargas was knocked backwards, stunned and barely conscious. Wheeler only took time to collect the man's second pistol before he turned and sprinted towards the ranch house, intent upon the man in the doorway.

It was a waste of breath, because as Wheeler reached him, knife in hand to counter any further arguments, the man gave a massive groan and slumped sideways.

'Cashed,' Wheeler offered, turning the body with a callous foot, only to spin round as the sound of hoofs announced the departure of the remaining bad man. Instinctively, Wheeler jerked up his borrowed revolver, then relaxed as the mounted bandit, plying his quirt for all it was worth, swept round the corner of the barn and headed across country, carefully keeping the buildings between him and the cold-eyed *gringo* who could shoot like the devil himself. Moments later, the man had topped a rise on the trail towards town and was seen no more. With a dissatisfied grunt, Wheeler turned back to the doorway.

'Miz Delia,' he began, apparently unperturbed at having killed or wounded four men in the space of half-a-dozen breaths, 'could you rustle up some hot water?'

'For that . . . thing?' she demanded, gesturing violently at the now unconscious Billy Vargas. 'Do you know what he had planned for tonight's *entertainment*? Do you? Do you? It was *me*,' she finished, voice rising hysterically with every word.

As usual, Wheeler didn't hesitate. He swung a hard hand, catching the girl solidly across the cheek and when she had brushed the tears of shock from her lashes she found herself looking into a pair of cold green eyes while a hard voice was saying, 'Now, you can stop right there. Oh, you're right,' he went on, as he saw her face begin to crumple again, 'they was sure set to rape and kill you and probably a lot of other things in between that you really don't want to think about. But they didn't and they're the ones dead and we're still standin' and that, young lady, is the only thing, the absolute only thing that counts.

126

And if you start in bawlin' like a sick dogie, I'm gonna whang you agin.'

'You're a real bastard, Cord Wheeler,' the girl snapped, 'but I still ain't doctorin' that Billy Vargas.'

'Never wanted you to,' Wheeler stated flatly, heading for the barn where he guessed the bandits' mounts were hidden. 'It's for your dad. He stopped a bullet and we did some hard travellin' gettin' here. I had to hide him up on the rim while I put on that l'il act to draw your company out into the open. Don't worry,' he finished over his shoulder, 'I'll take care o' your boyfriend.'

'What's wrong with just letting him bleed to death?' came the waspish response.

'No,' Wheeler said thoughtfully, 'I need him.'

Startled out of her fragile equanimity, the girl demanded, 'You need him? For what?'

'Bait,' came the brusque reply.

Underwood's wound turned out to be less serious than Wheeler had feared and he was sitting up in bed with his nurse fussing around him when the detective returned from hog-tying Billy Vargas to a convenient veranda post.

'Gagged and blindfolded too,' Wheeler finished, as Delia Underwood collected up the dinner dishes and headed for the kitchen. 'And since we're both here so nice and cosy,' he went on, 'suppose you tell me how it was that you come to be bossin' this collection of cat-house sweepings? Couldn't you get no good men?'

'They wasn't that bad,' Underwood bridled, 'it's

just you're better with a short gun than near anyone I've ever seen. Besides, they wasn't nothin' to do with me.

'Coupla years before I found this place,' Underwood began, 'when the kids' mother was still alive, fact is afore they were even born, I got in some . . . trouble. Shootin' trouble,' he admitted, anticipating Wheeler's question. 'The fella died and there was some question about where he was shot, so I naturally faded.'

'This was in N'Orleans before you left?' Wheeler asked, and Underwood nodded.

'Anyhow,' the old rancher went on, 'I thought I'd run far enough to get away from it but about five years ago, someone came to town who knew about me and the killin'. They blackmailed me into frontin' the rustlin' and there was nothing I could do about it,' he finished.

'Who was it?' Wheeler asked.

'I ain't sayin',' Underwood insisted stubbornly. 'S— they got somethin' else on me, somethin' I don't want the kids to know nothin' about.'

'It's all right, Cal,' Wheeler said mildly, 'you just told me who it was, plain as if you shouted it from the roof tops. Don't take it so hard,' he went on, gazing down mildly down at the badly disgruntled rancher, 'I'd just about worked it out anyway.'

'Huh, think you're smart, I guess,' Underwood snapped. 'When do we go to town and call this bunch's bluff?'

'Coupla days,' Wheeler said absently. 'How was your calf crop this year?'

'Good,' Underwood responded, clearly mystified at this apparently inconsequential change of subject. His curiosity, however, was left unsatisfied because all Wheeler said was, 'Good. Tomorrow, mebbe, you and me are gonna do a little business.'

If Underwood had felt himself confused that evening, it was nothing to the amazement that hit him, early next morning, when Wheeler presented him with a paper he had drafted in his clear flowing handwriting the previous evening.

'Hell, Cord, why don't you just take one, if you want it?' he demanded.

'Won't do,' Wheeler returned, shaking his head. 'They've got to be my property, otherwise it won't work.'

'Well . . .' Underwood began, but he was interrupted by his son's voice.

'Cord! Cord!' Lou Underwood bellowed, slamming through the bedroom door, to fetch up against the foot of his father's bed.

'There's a rider coming, up the trail from town.'

CHAPTER FIFTEEN

Within seconds, Wheeler was out on the porch, Gomez's Spencer cocked and ready under his arm.

Minute by minute the tension mounted, as the man from El Paso scanned the trail and the miniature figure grew to recognizable proportions. Then, Wheeler relaxed and passed the rifle across to Underwood.

'It's Sly,' he stated, 'I wonder what that ol' reprobate wants?'

'I see that sneaky l'il bastard Alfredo creepin' into town late last night. He was comin' from this direction so I figured I'd just drop in for a friendly visit,' the old man explained when Wheeler taxed him with characteristic cowboy rudeness about his presence.

'You allus go visitin' with a hundred rounds o' Winchester cartridges strapped round your gut and a spare Colt in the backstrap o' your Levis?' Wheeler asked.

'Allus,' the old man returned, without batting an eyelid. 'With friends, the rifle-stealin' bastards, like I got, you can't never be too careful. Bad though they are,' he added slyly, 'most of 'em at least offer a feller a drink.'

'No time,' Wheeler said, adding inconsequentially, as he turned away, 'How's your ropin' arm?'

'Things was sure peaceful around here afore you turned up,' Templeton sighed wistfully, following Wheeler towards the horse corral.

'We'll give you about an hour's start, Sly, which should give you plenty o' time to get back before we show up. I'll finish with l'il Billy an' then meet you outside the saloon. Don't forget, I don't want nobody to know we're back in town 'til I'm ready. *Sabe?*'

'Yeah, I got you,' the old cowhand snapped, 'on account of you barely told me more'n a dozen times. Now, you sure you don't want to tell it to me again?' he finished waspishly, before swinging aboard his barrel-chested grey mustang and booting home the Winchester carbine that Wheeler handed up.

'Keep your worthless head down,' the detective ordered, 'and Sly,' he finished seriously, 'don't waste no lead. These *hombres* play for keeps. Tell Jesse that too, when you see him.'

'Never met a Tejano yet that wasted anythin' that cost money,' the old man returned shortly.

With Templeton gone for nearly his allotted hour, Wheeler returned to the wagon that was to be used to transport Delia and her father to town, along with Billy Vargas, and the Bar U branded calf whose mother was securely roped to the tailgate.

Carefully, Wheeler checked the ropes, gag and blindfold that he had used to restrain the groaning

Vargas, then swung up on to Gomez's dainty palomino. Settled in the saddle, he swept a final glance over the ranch, then nodded to Lou Underwood, sitting his pony on the other side of the big wagon.

'Let's go to town,' the detective ordered.

Meanwhile, in one of the better rooms of Mariah Keely's boarding-house, Tyson and Abe Vargas were planning a small double cross.

'I gotta hand it to you, Marshal, you sure do write a neat hand,' Vargas rumbled, as he examined the document a worried-looking Tyson offered him.

'I don't like it,' the other returned. 'What happens when the boss finds out we got a will that leaves us Jase's ranch an' all?'

'Simple,' Vargas stated flatly. 'Then the boss won't be the boss no more. You and me'll be running things and the boss ... well the boss'll be workin' for us, 'cause this job don't work without the ranch to run the rebranded critturs on an' the brand that goes with it.'

'I dunno, Abe,' Tyson began. 'The boss ain't stupid and what about that detective fella, that Wheeler? He—'

'Ain't gonna be a problem,' Vargas finished impatiently, 'I offered Alfredo a hundred bucks to kill him on sight.'

'A hundred?' Tyson whined dubiously. 'That's good wages for a greaser to do a killin'.'

'Sure is,' Vargas admitted, 'if I was gonna pay him.'

'I still don't understand why we've gotta hole up like this,' Lou Underwood complained, as he finished roping Billy Vargas to a convenient post in the rundown little stable on the outskirts of town that his father had suggested for a temporary hideout, after their uneventful trip to town.

'Why can't we just go in and brace them coyotes?' the young man demanded.

'Like I told you,' Wheeler explained patiently, 'just because we know how they worked it and who done it, that ain't gonna stand in a courtroom. We got no hard evidence. Hell,' he snapped, uncharacteristically vehement, 'we can't even tie their boss to the rebranded cows we found on Elfords' ranch!

'No,' Wheeler continued, 'we gotta have proof and I think I know just the place to get it.'

'And just where might that be?' Delia Underwood demanded.

'In a lady's bedroom,' Wheeler admitted shamelessly as he stooped and put an eye to the rickety door. 'Don't forget to feed and water that cow. She's evidence.' Then he was gone into the swiftly falling desert twilight before anyone could think of a suitable retort.

Wheeler had reached the shadows across the street from the cantina, when a low whistle snapped him sideways, hand driving for Phillipe's long-barrelled Colt. Seconds later, he relaxed and pushed the pistol back into his belt as Sly Templeton appeared silently from the shadows.

'Somethin's up,' the old cowhand began without preamble. 'Tyson's got a grin like a yard o' oil and Vargas is buyin' drinks fer the crowd like it's goin' outa fashion. I hope you got somethin' good up your sleeve!'

'At the moment, just my arm,' Wheeler admitted. 'Although,' he added, turning into the friendly shadows, 'I hope to do better than that.'

'An' just how was you figgerin' to get in there?' Templeton demanded, as the pair surveyed the back of a neat, whitewashed house in the better part of Santiago.

'Brung the rope like I told you?' Wheeler demanded, as he slipped forward silently, apparently ignoring the other's question.

'Yes, I brung the rope—' Templeton began.

'Good,' Wheeler interrupted. 'Now see if you can put a loop over that chimney.'

The chimney was thirty feet up, in the dark, so not unexpectedly, Templeton's first throw missed, although not by very much.

'I bet the Bar U cows sure got a lot o' fun outa you,' Wheeler offered acidly. The old man grunted, easing the coiled rope through his gnarled hands, judging distance and the light breeze that had sprung up. Then, he threw; there was a soft slap and a grunt of triumph as the old cowhand pulled the rope tight.

Without a sound, Wheeler pulled himself upward swiftly and with an agile twist seated himself on the window ledge, the window having fortunately been left open. A couple of flips freed the rope and Wheeler dropped his end to the ground where Templeton coiled it lovingly before slipping back into the shadows.

With no more sound than a pack rat in a grain bag, Wheeler slipped over the sill, swiftly drew the curtains and surveyed the room he found himself in. It was obviously a sitting-room, elegantly appointed with a central table covered by an ornate tapestry which fell in symmetrical folds almost to the ground. Facing him across the table was a door, with a second opening in the adjacent wall.

A careful check showed that the first door opened on to a corridor, which clearly gave access to a number of other rooms. After listening a moment, Wheeler eased the door shut and silently wedged a chair under the substantial brass handle.

Through the second door was a bedroom, if possible even more lavishly appointed than the sitting-room. Ignoring the furnishings, Wheeler made a swift but thorough search, even turning aside the mattress, only to come up blank. He shrugged, never having really expected to find business records, especially this woman's business records, in her bedroom.

' 'Cause if anyone knows that bed an' business don't mix, she does,' Wheeler admitted, impressed despite himself.

Working more swiftly now, he began an equally exhaustive search of the sitting-room, but found nothing until he turned his attention to the pictures on the walls. The first two he examined were conventionally hung, but the third, a large portrait of horses drinking from a stream, refused to move. A moment's examination revealed a catch, let in halfway down the frame which when pressed, allowed the picture to be swung back to reveal a small but very substantial safe let into the wall.

'Fancy,' Wheeler muttered, eyeing the Brandenburg

patent combination lock with dislike. Even an expert would take a couple of hours to get past that lock and Wheeler, as he admitted ruefully to himself, was no expert.

However, before he could even reach up to touch the metal, the sound of raised voices suddenly split the silence of the room. In an instant, Wheeler had silently returned the chair to its original place and, after a single desperate sweeping glance around the room, had dived for cover under the ornate tapestry covering the table.

He was barely secure within his hiding place when he heard the door open and an angry feminine voice saying, 'Christ, Tyson, you're a fool. Wheeler's out-played you at every turn, you and Abe both and now you set some incompetent greaser to look for him. Ain't you got it yet? That bastard detective is tricky and smart and you can bet he's well on the way to figgerin' out everything.'

'Hell.' The whine in Tyson's voice didn't improve it. 'What we gonna do?'

'We?' the woman demanded. 'We? I don't know what you're going to do, Marshal, but I intend to sell up and move on. Wheeler may think he knows a lot but he can't prove any of it. Not without what's in that safe, at least,' she finished.

Tyson's expression must have clearly been disbelieving because after a moment, she snapped, 'Look, you stupid bastard, I'll show you.' Scarcely daring to breathe, Wheeler eased up the corner of the tapestry facing the picture as the woman swung it back. Both the occupants of the room were directing all their attention towards the safe and, hardly daring to believe his luck, Wheeler carefully memorized the combination as the woman twirled the dials.

Angrily, she jerked down the substantial brass handle but by the time she turned back to the table, presumably clutching the safe's contents, Wheeler was safely behind his tapestry.

'See?' she demanded waspishly. 'Everything's here. Receipts, payments, lists of buyers. the whole thing. All here and all safe. Destroy this and there's no proof the organization ever existed.'

'Hey,' Tyson began. 'I thought this was just a local job. You've got brands registered from here to the Canadian.'

'Why play for peanuts?' the woman said callously. 'But it ain't all my idea,' she went on unwisely. 'There's big people behind this, so if you or your little friend Vargas are plannin' some sort of double cross, I'd think again.'

There came a sound of paper shuffling and then a clang followed by a metallic click.

'Now you can get out,' the female voice said waspishly, 'I've got more pleasant things to do than look at your ugly face.'

The door was barely closed behind them, when Wheeler was out from under the table.

Minutes later, Sly Templeton heard the click of the building's rear door and someone whistling 'Shenendoah'.

As Templeton silently materialized at Wheeler's side, the detective shoved the burlap sack containing the papers and red Morocco account book into his arms before saying, 'Don't go nowhere. I've just got to go back upstairs for something.'

CHAPTER SIXTEEN

'Looks to be goin' well,' Vargas offered, shifting his elbow from the bar of Santiago's only cantina, to take a pull at the latest in a line of foul-smelling black cigars, which he had invariably accepted in lieu of a drink since the evening's entertainment had begun.

'Well?' Tyson echoed, pausing only to throw another slug of the raw frontier spirit down his throat. 'It's going great, Abe, ol' buddy, ol' pal, i's going jus' grea'. Purty soon this bunch'll be ready to hang their own mother, let alone Underwood, if he's fool enough to turn up.'

'Ease up on the liquor, you damn fool. We ain't outa the cow flop yet, not by a hell of a long way. Them boys don't look to be doin' much celebratin',' he finished, motioning with an outsize finger.

Following the direction of Varga's finger, Tyson felt the liquor drain out of him. Jesse Wrawlings and his son were sitting at a table with Baxter, the manager of the Circle R and Ramirez, the owner of the Bar B. Their crews were mingling amicably enough with the townsfolk, but their payday high spirits were missing and try as he might, Tyson failed to detect any one of the cowboys using the free liquor. Turning back to Vargas, Tyson opened his mouth to speak when something slammed back the batwings and a man stepped lightly through the opening.

For a moment no one moved, then Tyson dropped his hand gunwards.

'Wheeler!' he snapped, then stood very still, gun half drawn because a pistol was boring into his back just over his favourite kidney.

'Keep it comin', Marshal,' Jesse Wrawlings ordered with relish. 'Real slow and careful unless you want me to save the town the price of a rope.'

'This ain't gonna do no good, Wrawlings,' Tyson whined, as he watched Abe Vargas similarly divested of his hardware by Sly Templeton.

'This man,' he went on pompously, 'is a convicted felon, guilty of aiding the escape of a prisoner. I figger he's part of Cal Underwood's rustlin' set up, too,' he blurted.

'Well, Cord,' Wrawlings asked tightly, 'you bin swinging a wide loop?'

'Would I be working at jobs like this if I was?' Wheeler demanded with a grin, as he approached the bar, followed by the three Underwoods and a sheepish Billy Vargas.

'No,' the man from El Paso went on, abruptly sobering, 'I'm admitting here and now that Cal here was actin' as cover for the real criminals, but he was being blackmailed, so I guess it weren't his fault. But before we commence proceedin's, as the lawyer sharps say, we better have His Honour in here to

140

preside, and Mr Satz,' he went on, motioning to the young deputy, 'would you ask Miz Keely to step over here. Oh, and you might want this,' he finished, unpinning the tarnished star from Tyson's vest and tossing it across to the younger man.

'I don't understand why I've been forced to come here,' Mariah Keely mumbled, dabbing at her reddened eyes with a scrap of linen.

'I've never been in a saloon in my life. Mr Wheeler,' she went on. 'Why are you being so ungentlemanly as to force me to come here?'

The trace of New Orleans was strong in her speech to Wheeler's receptive ear and it swept away any remaining doubts he might have had. But he was all courtesy as he swept off his hat and said, 'If you'll have a seat, ma'am, I'm sure I can make it clear to you in just a few minutes.'

'Thank you, suh,' the woman responded coldly, moving to stand at the end of the bar, near the door, 'My father always said one should face your accusers standing.' Wheeler bowed again in response and moved to the centre of the sawdust-covered dance floor.

'I was hired by the dead man, Jase Elford,' he began without preamble, 'to come down here as his bodyguard, him claiming to be worried about a certain Cal Underwood, with whom he had some business.' Wheeler paused, glance sweeping the room.

'Of course,' he went on, 'as soon as I got here, I realized that Elford hadn't quite given me the straight of it. But then he got hisself murdered and it looked like young Lou might have been responsible.'

'What about the rustlin'?' Davy Wrawlings demanded. 'D'you find out about that?'

'Yep,' Wheeler nodded, and smiled swiftly at the young man to take the sting from his words. 'You an' your pa had no luck 'cause you was lookin' for the wrong thing in the wrong place!'

In a few words, Wheeler explained about the hidden canyon and the changed brands, indicating the alterations with pictures drawn in whiskey on the bar top. When he'd finished, Jesse Wrawlings pushed back his battered Stetson.

'How long you figger they been pulling this off, Cord?' he asked.

'About five years,' the detective answered easily. 'Thing is though,' he went on, 'none of it would have worked without the right person running it.'

'Jase Elford, surely?' Templeton returned.

'Him? Naw,' Wheeler stated flatly. 'He was just muscle. He'd never bought nor sold a cow legal in his life. He showed me that when he told me he'd taken Underwood's note for some cows Elford had sold him. I figger he did the hiring, brought in the crews and mebbe figgered out the routes. No,' Wheeler went on, 'there was someone a sight cleverer than Jase Elford bossing this set up. Only mistake they made was the way they killed him.'

In the silence that descended, Mariah Keeley's voice suddenly cut through like a shard of glass.

'And how would they have done that, Mr Wheeler?' she demanded.

'They poisoned him, ma'am,' Wheeler returned softly. 'Poisoned him with strychnine, just like the stuff in the bottle I found in your safe. Tell me, ma'am,' he said conversationally, 'would you prefer to hang as Keely or under your real name . . . Mrs Underwood?'

For a moment silence descended again like a pall, to be broken this time by Abe Vargas. Applauding.

'This is all real neat,' he sneered, allowing his hands to fall to his side, 'but so far you ain't got one spot of evidence.'

'And just what would you call evidence, Mr Vargas?' Wheeler returned.

'Cows, smartass,' came the sneering reply. 'Cows with the marks fresh on 'em.'

'Oh,' Wheeler said, 'you mean like the one I got outside, with the B H B mark still raw, even though she's suckling a Bar U calf ? You want someone should check, Mr Vargas?'

Davy Wrawlings was out in the street in an instant. One look at his face was enough to confirm Wheeler's story as the boy stopped in front of Vargas, his gun hand hovering over his pistol.

'Brand's been altered, certain as sunrise. What's the word, Vargas?'

The big man glared round at his younger brother, opening his mouth to speak. But he never got the chance.

Billy Vargas took one guilty look at the storm gathering on his brother's face and forgetful of time and place, forgetful of everything except his brother's towering rage, screamed, 'But it can't be, Abe! All them cows was healed afore we turned 'em loose. Just like you told me so someone'd find 'em and think Lou was brandin' mavericks!' Aghast at what he had just confessed, he backed away.

'No, I didn't mean that! It weren't my fault, Abe! Honest!'

'You heard enough, Marshal?' Wheeler asked.

'Sure,' Satz nodded. ' 'Nough to convict 'em both ten times over. But what about Miz Keely? Seems like you ain't got nothin' on her.'

'I don't think you'll see it that way when I show you all the account books and such I took from her safe,' Wheeler informed him. Turning to the woman, he asked, 'How about it, ma'am?'

'I told that fool you were too clever to be useful,' the woman said softly. 'How did you know I killed that slug?'

'Poison and a derringer.' Wheeler shrugged. 'It just yelled at me that the murderer was a woman. And,' he admitted ruefully, 'you called me "Mr Wheeler" that day I arrived before I'd even introduced myself. And who else could have searched my room that first night? And when I saw young Billy goin' in your back door an' you in that nightgown, well, ma'am, it all just added up.'

'How'd you know I was Cal's wife?' she demanded, shifting slightly to bring her face more into the light.

'Didn't know perzactly that you was,' Wheeler admitted. 'But I saw you an' Miz Delia standin' together the night Lou made his break and you two was so alike, it was plain you couldn't ha' been no one else but that girl's mother.'

'Oh God.' Mariah Keely suddenly erupted, tears welling in her eyes. Turning to Delia, she held out her arms and sobbed, 'Oh my darling, I've been such a fool!' It was beautifully done, and young and impressionable, Delia couldn't resist it.

Impulsively, she ran into her mother's arms even as Cord Wheeler screamed a warning and sent his hand driving for the long barrelled Smith & Wesson riding on his hip. But Wheeler was too late. Mariah Keely's left arm enfolded the girl an instant before Wheeler could line his pistol.

'Back off,' Mariah Keely snapped, turning her daughter slightly to show the cocked derringer pressed against her stomach. 'And you can give those fools back their guns.'

Without waiting for any further invitation, Abe Vargas snatched up his pistols from the bar and turned a furious face to Cord Wheeler.

'I oughta kill you,' the giant began, lifting a revolver. Wheeler's pistol jerked minutely.

'Go ahead,' the detective offered evenly. 'Pull and we'll ride to Hell together.'

'Vargas! Stop play actin' and you and Tyson get the hell over here,' Mariah Keely ordered. 'And what about that?' she finished, with a contemptuous jerk of her chin in the direction of a petrified Billy Vargas.

For a moment, the older Vargas fumed then he said, almost unwillingly, 'He's kin. Billy, get the scattergun from behind the bar and you, woman, get out front with that little bitch!'

As Mariah Keely edged past and through the batwings, Vargas shifted round to cover her, with the terrified Tyson scuttling alongside. With the two women safe in the darkness beyond the lamplight, Vargas hefted his two guns and confident of his domination of the room jerked his head at Tyson, before bellowing, 'Billy! Get over here!'

Swiftly, his younger brother joined him and with the sawn off now drawing the attention of the crowd, Vargas began to follow Tyson through the swinging doors.

He was almost through with Billy following close behind, when the left-hand door slipped from his massive shoulder and slammed forward, catching Billy in the back, causing him to stagger and swing the shotgun slightly off line.

Minute though the change was, it was advantage enough for two of the crowd. Wheeler's Smith & Wesson crashed an instant in front of Sly Templeton's old Remington, the detective's shot driving into Billy Varga's shoulder and propelling him backwards through the door into the moonlit dust of the street, while the old cowhand's .44 slug smashed into the sawn-off, destroying the breech mechanism.

As if driven by a single mind, every man in the place rushed the door, only to be forced back by a fusillade of shots from Abe Varga's revolver and a steely feminine voice saying, 'The first man through that door'll find a dead girl waitin' for him! Tyson,' the voice went on, 'find some horses and you, Vargas, shut that whinin' bastard up.'

Inside the badly lit saloon, Lou Underwood erupted.

'Christ, Cord, they got Delia and once they get horses, Christ knows where they'll get to!'

'Jesse, did you do like I told you?' Wheeler asked mildly, apparently indifferent to the boy's concern.

'Sure, Cord,' the big man rumbled. 'Got two o' my boys ridin' herd on 'em, coupla mile out o' town.'

'An' afore you ask,' Templeton snapped, carefully ejecting the spent cartridge from his treasured Remington, 'I got every other pony off'n every hitch rail while young Hooper was bringing that woman over here. Satisfied?'

'Sure you never missed none?' Wheeler demanded. 'Seems like it's your night for missing things,' he added slyly. Before the old man could explode, Wheeler said, 'Joshin' aside, we gotta get movin'. Sly, get your worthless old carcass out in the street and see where they go. An' keep everybody away from them. We don't want no more accidents.'

'I figger they'll make for the boardin'-house,' Templeton acknowledged shrewdly.

'Makes sense,' Wheeler admitted. 'But Sly, find 'em. We gotta get that girl out . . . and in one piece.'

CHAPTER SEVENTEEN

'I don't like it,' Abe Vargas rumbled, scanning the street, now lit by a faint dawn light, from the front window of Mariah Keely's boarding-house, for perhaps the twentieth time in an hour.

'It was too pat. First, no horses, then we get back here, without so much as seein' anybody. They must know where we are, so why ain't they done nuthin'? Besides,' he went on, 'we can't stay here. Three of us ain't enough to watch all the places they could get in, even if I had three good men,' he finished with a sneer.

Vargas glared round the big dining-room. Billy was lying in the corner, whimpering, the blood dripping sluggishly from his smashed shoulder to form a viscous pool on the worn carpet while Tyson hurried nervously from window to door and back again, clearly tearing his nerves to shreds. Delia Underwood was roped to a chair set against the back wall.

Of the five, Mariah Keely seemed the most

composed. She had occupied her time changing into shirt and Levis and as Vargas finished, she turned to him with a shrug.

'You're right,' she admitted without preamble. 'Looking at the whole thing now, it's obvious that this was planned. Wheeler intended us to be cooped up here and now he's got all the time in the world, while we're short of food and water.'

'Don't forget cartridges,' Vargas rumbled. 'We got one ace, though,' he went on, 'the girl.'

'But it's one we dare not play,' the woman explained patiently. 'What d'you think those men would do to you if you harmed that girl?' Seeing the understanding cloud Vargas' face, she nodded, before saying, 'Yeah! I wonder what that bastard detective's up to. Whatever it is, I bet he ain't been wasting his time.'

Mariah Keely was right. In the pre-dawn light, Wheeler had mustered his forces and carefully explained his plan and now, with the men of the ranch crews in position, he was crouched behind the clapboard corner of a building across the street from the Keely boarding-house, giving Hooper Satz some final words of advice and instruction.

'Don't get too close to 'em, boy,' he went on, handing the youngster a white towel with its attached pole.

'Just stand away from this here corner and be ready to duck back in quick.'

Satz nodded, licking suddenly dry lips. His hands were steady though, as Wheeler slapped him on a scrawny shoulder and said, 'You're a good man and you're due to be an even better marshal but if there's gun play, don't forget that tomato can. It ain't the man who draws first who wins; it's the man who picks his spot and then puts his first bullet plumb into it that'll come out on top.'

Carefully, Wheeler checked the sun, just barely peeping over the tops of the opposite houses.

'Give us ten minutes,' he ordered, then he was gone, leaving Hooper Satz to the longest wait of his life.

'How you figger to get in?' Templeton demanded, 'Even Vargas ain't stupid enough to leave a window open.'

'Once the boys start firing,' Wheeler said patiently, 'no one's gonna hear me bust a window.'

The pair had reached the back of the boarding-house by a roundabout route and now, as Wheeler eased up to inspect the window, they heard a shout from the main street.

'Won't be long now,' Wheeler offered, drawing his pistol with a satisfied grunt.

'That little bastard,' Tyson grated, as Hooper Satz waved his flag and yelled, 'Hey, in the house!'

Instantly, Tyson threw up his pistol only to find his arm dragged down by Vargas, who grated, 'Now, just wait a minute. Let's see what he's got to say!' Raising his voice the big man bellowed, 'What is it, Deppity? We're listening.'

Sounding a good deal more confident than he was

feeling, Satz replied, 'Let Miz Delia go and then come out with your hands up. You'll all get a fair trial. Them's the only terms we . . . I'm gonna offer.'

'Not good enough, not good enough by a damn sight. We want horses, water and grub and a long start. You better think about it 'cause in about a half-hour, I'm gonna start cuttin' pieces off this girl an' sendin' 'em out this window. Now git!' Vargas bellowed, lifting his Colt and sending a shot in Satz's direction.

As if that were a signal, the attackers' guns opened up, lead beating a tattoo on the sun-dried timber, sending the building's defenders diving for cover. After a moment, Vargas gave a crow of triumph and landed a kick on the cowering Tyson.

'Get up, you cissy,' he sneered. 'Them fools are shootin' high on account o' not wantin' to hit the girl. Get up, you fool—' he began, only to stop abruptly as he found himself staring into the bore of a Remington double derringer held in Mariah Keely's rock-like hand.

'I've been thinking, Mr Vargas,' she began. 'And I've come to the conclusion that our partnership should be, how should I say, eh . . . terminated. It's you those men want and while they're having their fun, I can get clean away. Oh, don't look so surprised,' she went on. 'I've had a horse in that little back house, with a saddle and bridle, since before I killed Elford.'

Concentrating on the big man, Mariah Keely failed to see the prostrate Tyson ease his revolver from its holster and in one abrupt movement swing it up and fire.

151

Caught high in the chest by the heavy .44 slug, the woman was slammed back against the wall, triggering the derringer and sending its slug harmlessly into the floor just as Cord Wheeler erupted through the door.

He took in the scene at a glance and his pistol was lifting, hammer earing back as a fighting mad Abe Vargas charged towards him, hands reaching to rip and tear.

Instantly sure of his aim, Wheeler squeezed the trigger, to be greeted by a dry click as the cartridge failed to fire. Barely in time, Wheeler threw up his right hand, bringing it free of Vargas's encircling arms and desperately slamming the butt of the Smith & Wesson into the savage bearded face.

He barely had time for one blow, before a violent jerk sent the pistol spinning from his hand to leave him at the big man's mercy. Remorselessly, Wheeler felt the grip tightening on his chest but despite the danger, his mind worked with icy clarity.

Stiffening his thumb, he gouged it mercilessly into Vargas's eye socket. The big man screamed, his grip momentarily slackening and that was enough for the man from El Paso.

Wheeler jerked backwards, throwing all his weight against the rustler's grip and managing to drive a knee up between the big man's legs. Vargas screamed again, this time releasing his hold, to lean forward clutching himself and retching, the retching turning instantly into a choking scream as Wheeler smashed a moccasin-clad foot into his throat. Vargas collapsed to the floor, to take no more interest in the proceedings as Wheeler broke one of Mariah Keely's substantial mahogany chairs over his head.

'You ain't perzacktly big on fair fights, are you, Cord?' Sly Templeton enquired mildly from the doorway, hefting his old Remington, which, seconds before, he had been trying to use to put a .44 calibre slug through some vital part of Abe Vargas's anatomy.

'Yes, I am,' Wheeler objected stoutly, 'I believe in a fair fight. 'Course,' he added, with a dry grin as he felt his still aching ribs, 'what I mean by a fair fight is one I win.' His glance swept the room, then, abruptly sobering, he snapped, 'Where in hell is that bastard Tyson and Miz Delia?'

'I'm sure sorry you an' me ain't gonna be travellin' together,' Tyson sneered at the girl whom he had dumped in a filthy corner of Mariah Keely's little outhouse, containing the dainty little pinto which was the boarding-house owner's personal mount.

'I'm sure we would have had a fine time,' he went on, trying to force the bridle between the teeth of the reluctant pony. 'But this here pony won't carry both of us. Goddamn it, open your mouth, you bastard,' he screamed, as the pinto, unused to such callous treatment, fiddle-footed sideways.

Being himself unused to horses, Tyson slammed a fist into the pony's mouth, causing it to rear backwards, screaming in pain, hoofs slashing the air.

Incensed by his inability to control the animal, Tyson snatched out a pistol, although to what purpose will never be known, because suddenly the door of the outhouse slammed back and Hooper Satz was framed in the opening.

For a long moment, both men looked into eternity, then with a scream that was one part rage and three parts fear, Tyson jerked up his gun and fired, the bullet slamming into the woodwork above the younger man's head, even as Satz drew and fired in one smooth, controlled motion, driving a bullet straight into the former marshal's chest. Tyson collapsed without a sound but Satz was still careful to turn his former boss on to his back and secure his pistol, although the spreading stain on the fat man's shirt and his rapidly glazing, staring eyes told their own story. Swallowing his revulsion, Satz turned to the girl.

And so it was that Cord Wheeler and Sly Templeton burst in to the little stable, seconds later, to find the girl sitting up, while Satz inexpertly applied a scrap of wet handkerchief to her temple.

'I thought Tyson was going to kill you, Hooper,' the girl was saying. 'Honest, I've never seen anyone use a gun like that! Oh, give me that handkerchief. And, it sure looks like your face could stand a l'il tidyin', too. Honest, Hooper, when was the last time you sewed on a button?' Wheeler and Templeton exchanged meaningful glances and withdrew to the big dining-room.

'I'm figgering he'll live to hang,' Wheeler concluded, having finished securing the groaning Vargas, now struggling back to wakefulness.

'Sure a shame about Miz Keely,' Templeton offered, moving across to the body of the prostrate boarding-house keeper. 'Sure a fine lookin'—' He was interrupted by a groan from the figure on the floor and turned abruptly to his companion.

'Cord, she's alive.'

Swiftly, the detective examined the badly wounded woman, before finally kneeling back with an emphatic head shake. Mariah Keely's eyes were open and she managed a smile as she saw Wheeler's expression.

'Get my daughter . . . please.' she whispered, hoarsely. 'There's a few things I'd like to straighten out.'

'Best get Miz Delia,' Wheeler ordered, hands busy with the woman's injuries. 'And see if you can find a slug o' whiskey,' he added to Templeton's departing back.

'Good idea,' the old cowboy returned callously, 'After this morning's frolic, I could do with more than a touch my own self.'

CHAPTER EIGHTEEN

'I want you to stay, too, and hear this, Mr Wheeler,' Mariah Keely began, lying back gratefully and grimacing at the taste of the whiskey. The liquor seemed to give her strength, however, and her voice was slightly stronger as she began her story.

'I was about eighteen, working in a cat house in N'Orleans,' she said hoarsely, 'when I met your poor stupid father. Oh, don't look at me like that, child,' she continued, as Delia made to draw her hand away. 'Your pa is a good man but he's like most men when they're in love; they go blind.' She paused, gathering her strength.

'He fell in love with me and convinced himself that it was my bad luck that I'd had to become a whore. Well, he also talked me into going away with him, but there was this other one . . .'

'The mayor's son?' Wheeler offered, then to save the woman's strength, he went on quickly, 'My friend Ira knows the head of the N'Orleans police department. His telegram was waitin' for me when I got back.'

'Well,' the woman went on, 'Abel was waiting for

us. He drew on Cal and his first shot missed and I shot Abel in the back with my hideout gun. 'Course, Cal thought he'd done it and he knew no one'd believe he hadn't murdered Abel so we ran. I left him soon after the kids were born and went back to whoring.'

'I owned the Golden Bell on Front Street in El Paso, 'til a couple of years ago. Then I met Jase Elford. . . .'

Suddenly, the woman's body was racked with a fit of coughing. There was blood on her lips as she looked up and rasped, 'For Christ's sake give me a drink.' For several long moments, she lay, letting the whiskey do its work.

'I knew Cal was doing well, somewhere down this way . . . and that the children . . . *my* children were grown up.' For a moment, the dying woman caressed her daughter's hand. 'So I figgered to use him . . . You were right . . . Mr . . . Wheeler,' she went on, turning to look at the detective, 'Jase was too stupid to be anything but muscle.'

'So why'd you have to kill him,' Wheeler demanded gently.

'Bad . . . luck . . . Mr Wheeler,' she gasped. 'He saw my . . . girl . . . and me together that day you saved her from her . . . pony and . . . he guessed . . . same as you.'

'And that's somethin' I still don't get,' Wheeler demanded. 'Why did Elford bring me down here? It don't make sense.'

'Cal had decided not to be blackmailed . . . anymore. Elford brought you down here because he was gonna con Cal . . . into . . . thinking that you was a detective from New Orleans, hired to find Abel's . . . murderer. He figured Cal'd try for you and you'd kill . . . him.' She smiled almost gently. 'Hearing you . . . anyone . . . could tell where you was from.'

'Very neat,' Wheeler admitted, 'and what about . . .'

But Mariah Keely held up a limp hand.

'No more questions,' she begged, 'now I just want to talk to my daughter.'

Returning ten minutes later, Wheeler found Delia Underwood weeping over the corpse of her mother.

Mariah Underwood was buried near the Bar U ranch house on a fine summer morning and about a week later, Hooper Satz was in his chair, sifting through a batch of wanted posters, when a familiar figure entered the now tidy office.

Satz took in the duster coat and the battered carpet bag, before coming round the desk, hand outstretched.

'Gonna miss you around here, Cord,' the young man offered.

'Naw,' Wheeler demurred, 'I'd just be in the way. 'Sides, I got people to see in 'Paso. Good luck with Miz Delia,' he offered mildly, turning to go. 'And don't forget what I told you. Pick your target and then go for it. And that don't just apply to shooting a Colt.'

'Afore you go,' the young man asked, 'there's still one thing I don't understand. Where in hell did you find that Bar U cow with the changed brand ? Billy musta been awful dumb to let that slip.'

'Not really.' Wheeler shrugged, as he surveyed the street. 'Me and Sly branded that cow the day before we came to town. Figgered Billy was too stupid to have checked what his boys had been doing. You watch that ol' reprobate,' he added, 'he's too handy with a running iron to suit me.'

Satz followed him to the door, looking after his friend as Wheeler limped down the street. Then his head jerked up and a broad smile lit his face.

Somebody, somewhere was whistling 'Shenendoah'.